THE RIVAL IN SOUTH AFRICA NOVEL

AN ONLY ONE BED ROMANTIC COMEDY

LOVE AND WANDERLUST
BOOK 3.5

LIZ ALDEN

Have you read the prequel short story,
The Night in Lover's Bay? See how Marcella met the crew of *Eik*
and started on her adventure. It's available for free on all
retailers.

Also by Liz Alden:

<u>The Love and Wanderlust Series</u>
The Night in Lover's Bay (free prequel short story)
The Fling in Panama
The Slow Burn in Polynesia
The Second Chance in the Mediterranean
The Rival in South Africa (standalone novella)
The Player in New Zealand
The Best Friend in Indonesia (free standalone short story)

<u>Aged Like Fine Wine Series</u>
Rosé with My Fake Fiancé
Riesling with My Roommate
Prosecco with My Professor
Cava with My Colleague

<u>Holiday Retellings Series</u>
Nutcracker with Benefits
Frosty Proximity

<u>Wanderlust Resort Series</u>
Beach Boss (free standalone short story)
Beach Resolution
Put it in Beach Mode

<u>Standalones</u>
The Boudoir Arrangement

To my husband, with whom I have many overlapping hobbies, and yet we are never in competition.

ABOUT THE RIVAL IN SOUTH AFRICA

First crush. First kiss. First nemesis.

As kids, Alex Boyd and I were best friends. Until my crush sparked a kiss and our friendship went up in flames. Years of flip-flopping between avoidance and antagonizing turned into... well, us.

Now, anything I can do, Alex can do better. Raise money for charity? Run a marathon? Sail a regatta? Alex is there and besting me.

I'm determined to keep him out of my blossoming new photography career. But thanks to our meddling mothers, Alex winds up on a safari in South Africa with me.

Same trip. Same tent. Same bed.

Things are about to get wild.

THIS BOOK WAS ORIGINALLY PUBLISHED IN THE HATE ME LIKE YOU MEAN IT ANTHOLOGY. THERE HAVE BEEN MINOR CHANGES.

ONE

I WAS THE CRANKIEST PERSON WHO'D EVER BEEN ON A superyacht in the Mediterranean. It was seriously poor form to feel this shitty while on a multimillion-dollar vessel docked in Malta, a party in full swing occurring on all three decks of the boat.

My boyfriend wasn't there. My father hadn't bothered to show up to watch the regatta, which I'd lost anyway. And as I stood on the bow of the superyacht *Themis* and listened to the party happening behind me, I admitted to myself that perhaps sailing wasn't going to be my forever thing.

While losing the regatta had stung, it hadn't hurt *that* much. The truth was, I'd picked it up on a whim—it was something my peers had occasionally participated in and something I thought would interest my father. The sailing today was fun; the weather was perfect for it, and I felt a certain satisfaction with myself over how seamlessly our team worked together.

But we'd still lost. And I didn't feel the disappointment I'd expected to feel. It was occurring to me that sailing wasn't something I was passionate about.

The worst part hadn't actually been the loss itself. I was

more upset that the team that came in first included my least favorite person in the world. Alex Boyd wouldn't even have gotten into sailing if I hadn't started sailing. All our previous rivalries could have been coincidences, but the coincidences were stacking up.

"Don't be a sore loser, Nikki."

I turned to face him, my arms already crossed to protect myself from the slight chill in the air. He stood next to the dessert display, wearing a suit that fit him perfectly, the jacket unbuttoned and his hands in his pockets.

The accusation cut through me, and I sucked in a breath of air. I was *not* a sore loser.

But Alex was the worst winner. He was competitive to a fault. This scenario had played out many times before. Alex, a last-minute entry invading whatever event I was participating in, always came to me afterward, wanting to break down the day and point out everything I did wrong.

A few years back, I'd secured a charity entry for the London Marathon to fundraise for a home care cancer society. After months of training and recruiting pledge donations, I had asked Natasha, Alex's mother, if she would be willing to pledge for me and if I could ask around at her company. She'd smiled and said, of course, and as she was filling out the paperwork, calmly remarked that she hoped I wouldn't mind if she pledged a little bit less to me than she did to Alex. That was how I found out that Alex had signed up to run as well.

The marathon had stung the worst because it wasn't about the running for me. It was supposed to be about raising money for charity. And yes, Alex did get more money pledged than me, which was great for the charity. But the questions afterward just made me feel less than.

What training program did you follow? I've been taking salt and electrolyte supplements an hour before the start. Did you? How long did you taper for?

I'd wanted to enjoy the fact that I'd finished and raised thousands of pounds for the organization, but Alex wouldn't stop hounding me. *What race are you running next?*

I'd known Alex since we were teenagers in secondary school. Sometimes I still looked for the old Alex, the one I first knew who was too tall, too nerdy for our cliquish school. But he grew into his frame, his looks matured, and, while we were still growing into the adults we would be someday, I could see that Alex was going to be devastating.

Would I be giving up sailing because I wasn't as passionate about it as I should be? Or would I be giving it up because Alex soured it for me?

I didn't want to tell Alex any of this. "I'm not being a sore loser. Just thinking about Ion."

Alex's eyes narrowed, just like I knew they would, at the mention of my boyfriend. We had known each other so long, and he knew exactly how to push my buttons. But I knew how to push his too. Ion was a sore spot of Alex's, though god knows why.

"Where is Party Boy this evening?" Alex asked.

"He's not a party boy," I rebuffed automatically, even though that was exactly why I wished Ion was here. He would have loved this party, and one of the things I enjoyed about him was his ability to make these types of events easier. He was gregarious and attractive, and people loved him.

Except Alex.

"He's totally a party boy. Come on, his Instagram feed is ninety percent partying and ten percent shots of him naked."

"It's *his job*." Okay, yes, Ion's Instagram could have done a better job of furthering his modeling career, but those *half-naked* photos were his job.

Alex ignored me. "You don't have anything in common. Case in point, where is he tonight?" He gestured out over the water, the site of the race, the party, the awards ceremony where I didn't win.

"Sounds like jealousy, Alex," I taunted. "You don't know how to relax and have fun. I'm shocked you stepped out of your office long enough to even train for the regatta."

Alex's face soured. "I have time to relax," he insisted.

"You are a workaholic, and you know it. Don't put down other people just because they don't have the same drive or ambition that aligns exactly with yours."

He stepped closer to me. Normally at an event like this, I have high heels on to somewhat make up for our height difference. Here on *Themis*, though, like most yachts, shoes aren't allowed. When I made the walk down the dock in my dress from *Pegasus*, my parents' yacht, to here, I'd worn thongs that I'd slipped off at the lazarette and added to the line of shoes on the deck. This meant I was quite a few centimeters short of my usual arguing height.

Alex's lips tipped up in a smug smile. "If I'm such a workaholic who doesn't have time to train, then how did I win?"

"Maybe if you hadn't hired my sailing coach out from under me."

The corners of his mouth shot back down again. "I didn't know," he said, scowling. "He said he hadn't heard from you in a week."

"I was on vacation with Ion."

He waved his hand, another *case in point*. And suddenly, I was tired. Tired of arguing with Alex, tired of my boyfriend and my father not being here, tired of not even knowing why I was doing things.

I put my hands up, palm out, just completely *done*. "You know what, Alex? Just forget it all. Seriously, I had a fun day, for the most part. Can't you just leave me alone?"

Alex took a step back from me. There was just enough space between him and the railing on the boat for me to get by, so I moved to slip through and escape.

"Nikki," Alex started, his tone softer. He reached out his

hand, grabbing my elbow, but at the same moment, my toe caught on the hem of my dress, the soft fabric stretching and causing me to stumble...right into Alex. We both went down, Alex letting out a soft grunt as he connected elbow-first with the table.

I thought, for a second, that we'd barely escaped disaster. Alex's hand still gripped my elbow, his other arm bracing against the dessert buffet. My chin had clipped his shoulder, and my body was pressed against his, our shocked faces staring at each other.

Alex's eyes widened.

And then the table collapsed underneath us.

We tumbled over into a horrific still moment when everything stopped moving. The table was flattened underneath us, desserts smushed by Alex's back. I had avoided the worst of it, somehow having twisted to land on top of him.

I scrambled away from the mess.

Alex sat up, a bewildered expression on his face. "What. The. Fuck."

Oh my god. Oh my god, oh my god. Our mothers were going to kill us.

Stunned, Alex got his feet beneath him and staggered to standing. He peered over his shoulder, and as he twisted around, I saw clumps of icing and cake and macarons studding his jacket.

"What the fuck, Nikki?"

My chin snapped up at his tone. "Excuse me?" I was flabbergasted. How could he blame me for this? "You grabbed my arm!"

"You literally fell on me! I was trying to apologize." Our voices were raised and started to draw attention.

"For insulting my boyfriend? That's been long overdue."

Alex slipped an arm out of his jacket and gritted his teeth. "This doesn't have anything to do with Ion, and you know it. You just can't accept that I won."

"It was an accident!" My voice came out high and shrill. This is exactly where I knew this would end up, why I should have gotten out of here while I could. "And I could stand it just fine if you'd stopped rubbing your win in my face all the time. Sailing was my thing, and you've got your spindly, grubby hands all over it."

He smirked at me. "And I'm better at it than you. Maybe if you spent more time with your sailing coach instead of that shitty boyfriend of yours, you might have done better," he hissed. We were toe-to-toe now, teeth clenched and bare feet grinding the pastries down into the deck.

"Fuck. Off. Alex," I said between my teeth.

"Nikki!" came my mother's voice. "What is the meaning of this? Stop this nonsense right now!" She stepped closer to me, delicately avoiding the mutilated desserts lest her dress be ruined, one of the yacht staff following behind her. "Seriously, I don't know what has gotten into you two."

Mum brushed an errant strand of hair out of her face and tugged her silk wrap tighter around her shoulders.

Alex's mother appeared from the other side. Her voice matched her gaze: disappointed. "Alex, obviously, we've let this feud between you two go on long enough. The award part is over, and dessert looks like it'll be delayed, thanks to you two. Apologize to the staff and go down to your room."

Alex bowed his head to our mothers. "My apologies, Mum, Ana." He tipped his head to the chef standing in the corner as well. "Sorry, Marcella." He glanced around the deck, eyes barely flitting over me, and was gone.

Mum turned to me and shook her head. "You're going back to *Pegasus* too. This is far too much disappointment for one weekend." Tugging my arm, Mum pulled me over to Alex's mother.

"Sorry, Natasha." I did feel terrible. Thank god we were out on the bow of the boat and not in front of everyone.

Natasha rolled her eyes. "I can't believe you two are

twenty-four years old and we have to send you to your rooms like children," she said as I picked up my hem, now weighed down with the remnants of the dessert table.

I kept my eyes down, quickly walking back towards the stern. I'd nearly made it to the gangway when I hesitated. The regatta had been a team effort, and my coaches and fellow sailors were still having a good time. I at least owed them my thanks and a goodnight.

In the corner, I grabbed napkins from the table and did my best to clean off my feet and the hem of my dress. Weaving through the party, I found most of my crew mates and said goodnight, playing up how tired I was and letting a few very real yawns slip out.

I saved the regatta organizer for last, but unfortunately, Alex had just turned away from saying goodnight to Jack. He'd cleaned up, too, losing his tie and socks and unbuttoning his shirt.

We both stopped, eyeing each other, a heavy silence between us.

Alex broke it. "I have just one question. Is Ion the one?"

I drew back, surprised. "What?"

"You've been with him for nearly a year. You'd know by now if he was the one you were going to marry and spend the rest of your life with. Tell me he's the one for you, and I'll leave him alone."

My mouth hung open, poised to declare...what? He was? He wasn't? It was none of Alex's business? But nothing came out.

Because I didn't really know.

Instead of teasing me or making some cutting remark like I expected, Alex frowned, a crease forming between his eyebrows. And something, some spark, passed behind his eyes.

He shook it off. "Fine, whatever. Goodnight, Nikki."

I watched as Alex faded away into the party. Just because I

wasn't in love with Ion right now didn't mean I wouldn't be. Who was Alex to judge me? And why did I let him get to me so much?

I finished my goodnights and left the party, waffling back and forth about my own feelings over Ion, over sailing, over Alex. In my cabin on *Pegasus*, I checked my phone. I had several messages from Ion consoling me, plus a few pictures of him from the photo shoot today.

ION

Hey, babe, can you post these ones on Instagram and work your magic?

I smiled. So what if I wasn't in love with Ion yet? He was gorgeous and attentive, even if he wasn't here in person. And he didn't pick fights with me.

Relieved to have something to do to get my mind off the evening, I got to work editing the photos and writing the captions.

And I made a vow to myself: I'd never let Alex compete with me again.

TWO

Eight months later

Bigger is better, at least in this case.

But not too big.

I usually could work with one hand pretty well, but in this instance, I was definitely going to need two. I was a bit worried that my arms would get tired or I'd cause some damage. I had to choose one; I couldn't really fit two. And three would just be mad.

I looked at the options on the bed waiting for me. The biggest one was probably out.

That left the smaller option and the middle option. They both were heavy in my hands, a nice solid weight and some impressive girth.

My usual was about 250 mm, but these were much bigger.

I knew that I might regret not taking a big enough camera lens to South Africa with me. I sighed and picked the middle one up off the bed, then rearranged the padded dividers in the backpack to accommodate it. This was going to be my first time photographing on a safari, and the pressure was on. I had to get this right.

Just two months after the regatta in Malta, I quit sailing for good. I worried that I was leaving it behind for all the wrong reasons—Alex didn't get a say in what I did—but something else quickly took over my life.

I thought sailing would be my passion, something that excited me and gave me a sense of self. But I *know* that is what photography is for me.

It had started with Ion. After a few times editing and posting photos for him on his Instagram page, he handed over the entire account to me. And then his website and his portfolio and his modeling career started to take off. Whether the shot was a black-and-white close-up of Sunday morning in bed—tastefully naked—or lounging by the pool in sponsored wear, I was the one behind the lens. My shots weren't amazing—I was not a portraitist—but they were better for his career than what he'd been posting.

Six months later, I was diversifying, running my own social media campaigns and looking for sponsors. While I love all photography, the real spark had hit me with travel photography. Ion and I had realized that the romance was gone and amicably split.

The breakup didn't bother me. I was flooded with new excitement, real passion. I pushed myself further, taking courses and experimenting with different styles, and discovering new ways to record the world.

And now I was packing for my first FAM—Familiarisation —trip, where I was photographing a new South African safari lodge for their promotional materials. I'd get a complimentary stay at the resort in exchange for the use of my images.

I was just about done packing all my photography gear in the backpack—spare batteries, a wide-angle lens, filters, et cetera—when Tchaikovsky's "Sleeping Beauty Waltz" filled my room.

That was my mother's ringtone. No one else called anymore, anyway. Texts only, please. And she had been calling more and more lately as we got closer to my trip. She was nervous, and I understood. As far as she knew, I was traipsing off on vacation alone, not taking a work trip.

"Hello, Mum," I answered the phone.

"Nikki, darling, how is packing going?" My mother had a heavy Russian accent, one that she had coached out of my mouth early on. It was especially strong now, as it often was when she was emotional, and I knew this call would be tough.

"It's good. I'm just about done packing my camera gear, and I had to make some tough choices, but I think I'm ready."

She hummed on the line, and there was a small silence that had my heart rate picking up. *What now, Mum?*

"I think it's just awful you couldn't find anyone to take Ion's spot."

It wasn't that I couldn't find anyone to go with me on a most-expenses paid trip to South Africa. Sure, after Ion and I broke up, I did ask my best friend Harper if she wanted to come, but she already had a commitment. I could have asked around more—I was sure my cousin would have loved to join me, or, if I offered to pay for flights, some of my friends from uni would have jumped at the chance.

But I kind of wanted to go by myself.

This wasn't a usual trip. Rather, this was the start of something big for me, something I hoped to focus on and nurture for a week in the wilds of Kruger Park. I hadn't really shared how big this was with my mother. I loved her, but she took little interest in my activities beyond their social status. And if I wasn't exhibiting in galleries, my work probably wasn't of much interest.

And I didn't want her to tell Alex's mum.

"I'll be fine, Mum."

"But it's *Africa*." She said it like I was putting myself in grave danger, a military mission or a stroll through the streets of Birmingham at night. Never mind that she has just lumped an entire continent of diversity and beauty into something negative. Add in that my mates and their parents had been going to South Africa for ages on holiday, and she was really just panicking over me being alone.

Mothers aren't always rational, especially mine.

"I'm going on a safari. I'll be in the airports until the accommodations pick me up, and then I'll be on their campsite the entire time. There will be expert guides, and this place is really, really posh."

And it would be. I was stunned that I could convince the marketing team of one of the most luxurious, newest safari setups in southern Africa to give me a comped trip. It could be huge for me and, I hoped, for them.

"Well, there is good news. I have a solution."

My hand froze over my rolled-up hiking pants. This was not good.

"You'll never guess who's in dire need of vacation time."

I closed my eyes. *Oh no. Mum, just...no.*

"Alex!"

My mother said it with such excitement. Despite everything she's seen, the way Alex and I fight and argue, my mum *still* has it in her head that Alex and I would make a perfect couple.

Part of it, I know, is that my mum felt isolated when we moved to London. She didn't speak much English, and my six-year-old brain caught on faster than hers did. Aside from the church, Mum hadn't had many friends.

Until I met Alex. Mum and Alex's mother, Natasha, attended a parents' night at our secondary school and had clicked right away, despite being complete opposites. Natasha was a tech mogul, my mother a socialite.

They were both thrilled when Alex and I spent time together as teens. But after hormones kicked in, Alex and I fell out, and our mums were genuinely baffled by the idea that Alex and I didn't like each other anymore.

"Mum…" I tried to sound patient and not so entirely put out. I didn't want to offend her, and I definitely didn't want her to get any ideas in her head. Sometimes, I swear, the harder I rebelled against my mother's idea that we would make a great couple, the harder she dug her heels in. "Alex does not want to spend a week on safari with me. Besides, he'll probably be bored or thinking about work the entire time."

I hadn't seen Alex since Malta, but I'd heard through my mum that he'd been promoted again, having moved up to management at Natasha's company. If I really wanted to push Alex's buttons, I could just throw around the word "nepotism." It drove him mad, which I had to admit was a little mean. But also, fun.

Alex was *very* good at his job. And he obviously loved it. He had a special bond with his mum, and it made my heart ache that my mum and I weren't as close.

On top of that, Alex inherited a lot from his mum: he had his mother's looks, dark hair, deep brown eyes, and her drive and work ethic. As a teenager, I'd seen them bond together over Alex's early programming successes. Someday, no doubt, he'd be running the business she'd started when she was scraping together funding and trying to immigrate from Malaysia to England.

My parents had never shown much interest in anything I'd done, and my inheritance was in a trust fund.

"There's no Wi-Fi on the safari," I told Mum. "He won't be able to work at all."

"Perfect. That's exactly what he needs, a break from work," Mum said. "Can you believe he hasn't used any leave this year?"

I tried a different tactic. "Natasha would really give him that time off? He's so integral to her company." Natasha loved having her son work in the business with her.

"She's the one that suggested it."

"I don't think he'll be able to get a tent this late, Mum," I said. "I leave in two days, and I'm pretty sure they're only operating at a soft opening right now. Not all of the accommodations are ready yet."

"Oh, he'll just stay with you."

That actually caused me to sputter. "Mum! This is a safari. Yes, it's a high-end one, but there's only one bed!"

"Well, then, I guess you'll have to share. You are both grownups. This isn't a teenaged sleepover."

I rolled my eyes at that. I don't think I had a sleepover once as a teenager. Mum was watching too many American movies.

I tried to argue more, but Mum cut me off. "Рыбка," she said, and then I knew I was sunk. She only called me her little fish when she was serious and concerned. And also, she switched to Russian. It was a double whammy. "It would really make me feel better about you going on this trip."

I sighed and closed my eyes. What was that expression? How do you eat a cow? One bite at a time. The first bite was appeasing my mother. I would figure out the rest of the details later.

"Okay, fine, Mum, Alex can come. I'll ask him." Maybe I could just conveniently forget to talk to Alex, or we could both agree that it would be better to worm our way out of this than to actually go on a trip together. I couldn't imagine that Alex was too keen on taking a trip with me.

"Oh, dear, there's no need to ask. Natasha's already booked his flight for him, and she's talking to him right now. Just imagine how that conversation is going." She gave a tinkling laugh into my stunned silence. "Kisses, рыбка, I love you."

And she was gone.

———

WHILE PACKING, I MULLED MY PROBLEM OVER.

Fact: Alex was coming with me on this trip.

Also, fact: Alex could not know the real reason I was there.

Final nail-in-the-coffin fact: It would be next to impossible to hide.

I looked at the camera backpack, and the features and accessories that had once made me so happy now seemed to scream, *You're trying too hard!*

The last thing I wanted was Alex critiquing my every shot. He was always all too willing to offer "helpful" feedback, which would just drive me bonkers.

I could picture him leaning over my shoulder. *What if you tried a different aperture? Why didn't you pack a bigger lens, Nikki?*

I thought about switching the medium zoom lens out. I could go smaller—try to attract less attention—or I could go bigger.

Male inadequacy issues? *Compare yourself to my giant lens and feel lesser.*

I shook my head. I would *not* let Alex ruin this for me before it even got started. He probably didn't know much about photography, anyway. As smart as he was, his focus was narrow; I doubted aperture was even in his vocabulary.

Besides, it's not the size; it's how you use it.

As I rolled and packed my things—the hiking gear I bought before my Chichén Itzá trip and then used a dozen times over, the layers I was going to need on the cold nights, my travel-sized toiletries—I tried to work out a solution. The other option, one that changed little, was to be furious at my mother.

But eventually, my clothes were packed, and I still hadn't come up with a good idea. I moved over to the bathroom and pulled out some supplies for the evening's activities. There was no way I was going to bother packing a slew of things I didn't truly need, so I performed my pre-trip ritual. I washed my face, cleansed it, and applied a mask. Later, in the shower, I'd shave my legs and pits and bush so I didn't have to pack a razor or shaving cream.

I took a bottle of acetone out from behind the mirror and settled in to take my nail polish off and trim my nails.

Unfortunately, my recent thoughts of Alex combined with the acetone made my mind wander to the first time I had ever talked to him. We had gone to the same private school and had vaguely known each other in passing. One day, I stayed late—I don't even remember why anymore—and in passing through the empty halls, I found some graffiti on a locker. I knew whose locker it was just from the words sprawled across it: racist Asian bollocks with male genitalia commentary thrown in.

Furious, I'd stalked down to my own locker and dug out a bottle of acetone, the small travel kind, and cotton balls. I hoped it would be enough.

Alex was the only Asian kid in our school. He was lanky and a bit nerdy, and he hadn't grown into his long and lean body just yet. Of course, bullies in secondary will pick on anyone. I'd been called Horse Teeth for a while because my front two teeth are kind of big, but when my tits grew in, the nicknames no longer focused on my teeth. Calling me Knockers instead was ever so clever.

"What are you doing?"

Alex's voice rang out behind me as I was scrubbing off the "i."

"What does it look like? I'm shoving love notes in your locker, obviously."

A moment of silence stretched as I moved on to the "n." I heard Alex shift behind me, and wondered if he knew what had been written. Had he seen it already?

"Well, thanks."

His tone was resigned, so clearly not the first time this had happened.

"Pleasure. Won't give these wankers the satisfaction of everyone seeing this tomorrow. What are you doing here, anyway?"

His clothes rustled as he shrugged behind me. "Tutorials." He paused. "I'm the one getting tutored in maths, not the other way around."

"Didn't think you were. I remember your test scores."

"Yes, well, just wanted to make sure the day wasn't chock-ablock full of Asian stereotypes." After a moment of silence, he said, "I'm not even Chinese."

"Bullies don't tend to excel at geography." The "k" came off easily, and I capped the bottle and turned around.

He watched me, pursing his lips.

"What?"

"It's weird to hear you say wankers in your posh accent."

"Other people here have posh accents."

He tilted his head. "Not quite as posh as yours."

Alex's accent was muddled. As I learned later, his mother spoke with a slight Malaysian accent, his dad's accent was a rougher Cockney, and Alex ended up a hodge-podge. My accent, on the other hand, was metaphorically beaten into me. When our family moved from Russia—much to my mother's anger; it is something my parents still row about—my parents hired an elocution coach to help me fit in.

From that day on, after scrubbing the graffiti off his locker, Alex became one of my best mates. Until my teenaged hormones kicked in and threw everything off balance.

THREE

I sat in the Johannesburg airport at one of the high tables with a plug that miraculously turned it into a workstation, cramming at the last minute. I was nervous, and when I got nervous, I got compulsive. The compulsion had led me to obsessively reread emails and simultaneously watch YouTube videos.

While an American droned on in my ears about depth of field and focal points, I scanned an email from Siviwe, the marketing manager of Amukela Lodge.

We're operating on a soft launch right now, so only half the tents—six will be in use while you are here. The pool is fully functional, but the hot tub is not. As you can see from our website, we don't have much in the way of photographs yet, and that's where you come in.

We'd messaged back and forth after that, coming up with a list of shots to get beyond the obvious ones; staff photos, shots of the kitchen and rooms, plus all of the excursions.

I was going to be working my arse off for this luxurious "vacation."

Something touched my shoulder, and I pulled a headphone out, spinning in the chair and expecting to find someone asking if they could use the extra plug at my station to charge their phone. Instead, I spun right into Alex, who was leaning over my shoulder and looking at my laptop screen.

Thanks to my chair's height, I was eye-to-eye with him when my knee connected with his groin. It was an accident. Completely accidental.

But *so* satisfying.

Alex bent over with a soft grunt, and his hand reached out, attempting to keep himself upright. It happened to land on my knee, and he was lucky I didn't push him off. I was too busy tilting the screen of my laptop so he couldn't see anything else.

"What were you doing? Sneaking up on me? Snooping over my shoulder?"

Alex's hand was hot through my trousers, his fingers curled around my thigh. It reminded me of how he used to squeeze hard just above my knee back when we were school-mates, guaranteed to make me squeal and wiggle away. Casual, harmless flirting.

He sucked in a deep breath. "I was *not* snooping...." He trailed off at the sharp eye I gave him. "Okay, fine, I was snooping. You were looking so intently at the screen, and I have no idea what you've been up to lately."

"Maybe there's a reason for that."

Alex stood, removing his hand from my knee. "Come on, Nikki. I'm sorry."

I pursed my lips.

"Didn't kneeing me in the stones make up for it?"

I fought a smile, then rolled my eyes and sighed. "Fine. Go grab a seat at the gate. I'll pack up and meet you there."

He glanced over at the gate where there were half a dozen people spread out around the hundred or so black leather chairs. "I'll wait."

I slipped off the chair and pulled my headphones out of the jack, forgetting that the video was still playing.

"—BOKEH EFFECT, YOU WANT TO SET YOUR APERTURE AS WIDE AS IT WILL GO."

I scrambled to open my laptop and navigate around the thirty tabs I had open to find the YouTube video that continued to blare. Heads turned. Conversations stilled.

Ugh. I was *that* person.

I cut off the guy as he was espousing his favorite fast lenses. "Sorry. So sorry," I said, making eye contact with a few nearby people who'd been disturbed. My cheeks were radiating heat, and I carefully packed my stuff up while taking deep breaths, willing my face to cool down faster.

I slung my backpack over one shoulder and stalked past Alex, refusing to look at him. He picked up his bags—a sensible but new backpack and duffel bag, I noticed—and sullenly slumped into the chair across the aisle from me. I was often the receiver of Alex's broody stares, a look he perfected in secondary school after that fateful first kiss of ours.

I ignored him.

"Still helping Ion with his Instagram, I see."

"I'm not—" I stopped myself. If Alex wanted to believe I was researching photography for Ion's Instagram, I wasn't going to dissuade him from that idea. "Bokeh is very popular on Instagram right now." That was true.

Alex crossed his ankle onto his opposite knee. "So, what are you doing now, Nikki? Aside from helping Party Boy?"

Crap. I really should have come up with some kind of story. I hardly wanted to tell him I was filling my days with photo shoots and online lectures. Maybe I should be taking a class on subterfuge.

"Helping my mum out."

"With what?"

"Church?"

An eyebrow quirked. "Is that a question or an answer?"

The question is will you believe that, and the answer is no.

I sighed. "Neither."

We had a few moments of awkward silence where I looked anywhere other than Alex. Kids ran around, people coughed, talked on the phone, bought overpriced candies and boring paperback novels.

"Still running?" Alex asked, forcing my eyes back to his.

I bristled. "No."

"Sailing?" he inquired.

"No."

"What *are* you doing nowadays?" He steepled his fingers together.

I smiled. "Absolutely nothing."

"Aw, that's no fun."

"No, it isn't."

He blinked at me before changing the topic. "You and Ion broke up."

"Yes."

"He seems to be doing pretty well now."

Ugh. Just. Ugh. Sure, Ion and I had split up amicably, but Alex had always been so sure that Ion and I weren't right for each other. They'd never gotten along, with Alex leaving passive-aggressive comments on Ion's Instagram.

Looks like quite the party.

#partyboy

I hope Nikki's having fun with you.

Ion tended to just laugh them off. But he didn't know Alex well enough to hear that smug tone.

"I saw that video that went viral," Alex continued.

I knew exactly the one he was talking about. It was behind the scenes at a nude photo shoot. Ion was laughing, drinking what *might* be water, and his arse was on display. And it was *spectacular*.

Sure, we broke up, but for Pete's sake, I dated a model. I was allowed to miss his ass.

I wanted so badly to brag to Alex about my hand in Ion's career, but I kept my mouth shut. He'd either mock my hard work or, worse, become interested in it.

"Alex, you're just here to keep my mother happy. Enjoy the free trip, and keep your nose out of my business."

He tutted. "That's no way to speak to your travel buddy. We're going to be together twenty-four-seven for the next week. Let's at least try to make it civil."

Our section was called over the intercom, and I slung my backpack back onto my shoulders. "We can be completely civil, Alex." And I cut him a smile, as sweet as I could make it.

———

THE KRUGER MPUMALANGA INTERNATIONAL AIRPORT WAS TINY, completely outdoors, and surrounded by the scrub brush typical of the region. It was early afternoon when we landed, and our driver was easy to find—he held up a sign with my name on it. He introduced himself as Riaan and loaded our bags as Alex and I settled into the back seat of an open-air Jeep for the drive to the lodge.

The air was arid and warm, the bushes around us mostly devoid of leaves. It was approaching the dry season here, the best time to explore Kruger Park on account of the animals not being able to hide in the bushes. Watering holes, too, were few, and the animals tended to congregate there.

It was winter in the southern hemisphere, and while warm, it wasn't uncomfortable. The drive was pleasant, and Riaan chatted over his shoulder, telling us all kinds of information about the park.

Alex peppered him with questions, mostly things I already knew: Kruger Park was the largest park in Africa, we were practically guaranteed to see the big five—elephants, lions, leopards, rhinoceroses, and cape buffaloes—and when

Riaan mentioned speaking four languages, Alex begged him to teach us a few words in Afrikaans or Xitsonga, the local languages.

I watched Alex, bemused. Since we left school for different unis, most of our interactions had been around parties or our mutual friends or, as of late, our parents. I don't recall ever having seen this side of Alex, chumming with locals and putting that brain of his to good use.

I hid a smile behind my hand as Riaan taught him some slang and Alex fumbled with the pronunciation. Though I didn't enjoy spending time with Alex, and I have no idea why he agreed to come on this trip, his enthusiasm was contagious.

As the landscape passed by, my mind wandered back to the task at hand. We were drawing closer to the camp, and it struck me how remote we were. I ran over my packing list again in my head, praying that I hadn't forgotten anything critical. I wasn't alone in the physical sense, with Alex here beside me, but the added pressure of having Alex on this trip and of trying to stun the resort with my work at the same time was building butterflies up in my stomach.

"Nikki?"

Alex was watching me, and I released my lower lip from between my teeth.

Our Jeep slowed, and Riaan stuck his arm out the window and pointed out to the left where a small lake was coming into view. "Hippos."

"What, really?" Alex leaned toward me to get a better view. As we came to a stop, I could make out that what I had thought were wet rocks were actually hippos. They lazed about on the banks, occasionally flicking their tails or ears. White birds dotted the mud and hippo flanks, and Riaan explained they were eating bugs and pests from the hippos' skin.

When I turned back, Alex's face was right in front of me.

His eyes were wide, a grin crinkling his eyes and cheeks. I'd always liked the way his lips looked: rather thin, with delicate skin.

His eyes flicked to me and then back out the window. I turned my attention back to the hippos. "Most dangerous animals in Africa, I understand," I said.

"Yes," Riaan confirmed. "They are aggressive and cause too many road accidents. They are tanks."

When we'd had our fill, Riaan sped back up again. "Don't worry, you'll see plenty more," he assured us.

A few minutes later, he slowed again. Alex and I both leaned toward the center of the car, peering through the windshield. Ahead of us, stock-still on the road, stood a rather large hoofed animal. The coat was a glossy grey over rippling muscles, but the eyes were drawn to massive, spiraling horns. As we slowed, the beast—a kudu, Riaan said—leapt gracefully over the fence on the right side of the road, easily over two meters high.

Alex nudged my shoulder with his. Our eyes met as Riaan sped back up.

"I know you aren't keen on having me here."

"That's...I..." I floundered.

"Regardless, thank you for allowing me to come along." He wiped the palms of his hands against his thighs. "I know I haven't said thank you yet. But sincerely. Thank you."

My mouth hung open as Alex turned back to look outside the window. When was the last time Alex had thanked me for anything?

His honesty also made me realize that regardless of how the job went, I was here for the experience too. I needed to appreciate this opportunity that I had been given.

Riaan pointed through the treetops to a herd of giraffes off in the distance. Thoughts of my job disappeared, and I laughed when Alex imitated a giraffe's tongue. The flutter of excitement grew stronger with every kilometer we drove. This was Africa, and I couldn't wait to see it.

"So, there's only one bed?" Alex asked, peering around our tent.

To be fair, it was a huge bed. And the tent itself could hardly be called a tent. The bed was the focal piece, a king-sized, four-poster monstrosity with mosquito netting tied back with straps of canvas. The floor was concrete, the roof of the tent canvas with gossamer walls hanging down on all four sides. A light breeze blew in, and the curtains swayed. We had a small couch, a desk, and some upholstered chairs. At the foot of the bed sat a massive travel trunk for us to store our belongings to keep them out of the hands of the local troublemakers—monkeys.

"Only one bed. Did your mother not tell you that?" I asked innocently.

"You knew?"

I looked at him, eyebrows raised. "I did, and I still agreed, out of the kindness of my heart, to allow you to join me anyway."

"As in, your mum got to you."

"Of course she did."

Alex looked at the couch. Actually, one could hardly call it a couch. It was more of a loveseat. He looked back at me.

"This is my trip," I said primly.

"I will definitely not fit on this couch."

I crossed my arms, shifting my hips to lean against the couch in question. "Neither will I."

Alex took a few steps towards the front of the tent, the sunlight streaming in and highlighting motes of dust in the early afternoon light and backlighting him. "I'll ask them if they have another tent available."

"They don't." His eyebrow raised further, and I weighed my choices. How much should I tell him? "This is a soft opening. Not all of the tents are finished, and I do happen to know all the tents that are done are full."

Alex was silent for a moment, and the noises of the bush filtered in. Birds and insects sang while Alex chose his words carefully. "Fancy. How did you hook an invitation to this place?"

I shrugged noncommittally, trying not to get defensive. "I know people."

His face soured. "People like Ion, right?"

"No, he was not my connection. I got this one all by myself, thank you very much." I scowled at him. "I don't have to depend on a man for everything."

Alex returned my scowl but didn't argue. "So," he said, gesturing at the bed, "what are we going to do about this?"

"There's nothing to do. We're both grown-ups, and that bed is huge, even for you. Now, we have an hour until the afternoon drive starts, so I'm going to clean up a bit."

I gathered up my toiletry items and stepped into the bathroom block at the back of the tent. While Amukela was certainly luxurious for glamping, it was still glamping. The bathroom was a concrete and brick rectangular room at the back of the tent. The ceiling was open to the rest of the tent, and the doorway contained only a small drapery to block the view.

I set my things on the counter and looked over the space. A lovely tiled shower stall with a rain shower head was on one side, and to the other was the toilet. In front of me was a large mirror, a counter with a modern basin, and a small wooden chest. Curious, I opened the complicated latch and found the chest filled with standard hotel toiletries one would expect—top-shelf brands and very fine face flannels.

I moved the small toiletries to the shower and stripped out of my clothes.

"Is it just the one room in there?" Alex's voice, even at a regular speaking timber, rang out clearly.

Even though the curtain was closed and I was sure Alex wouldn't barge in—he'd never been *that* big of an arse—I covered my nips up, self-conscious enough just from hearing him.

"Just the one. Privacy, please." Before he could respond, I turned on the water in the shower. I knew that water was a limited resource—conservation signs were everywhere—so I hopped in quickly, rinsing the day of travel off my body. To my surprise, the water warmed up immediately. There must have been an instant water heater.

Once bathed and dry, I pushed the curtain aside and stepped into the room. I should have remembered to bring clothes in with me, but when I looked to the side, Alex was passed out on the bed, mouth slightly open and his lanky limbs sprawled out on the duvet.

FOUR

dressed for the afternoon drive in loose, pocketed shorts and a long-sleeve top. When I had first come out of the shower, Alex had been on his back on his side of the bed but had since migrated to the middle and had pulled a pillow in and hugged it tightly. Some would have called it adorable.

Some.

He blinked awake and, like a cat, stretched his arms up and over his head and then out in front of him. In fact, he looked remarkably like my mother's cat. The one who liked to lick himself and stare at you smugly. Hopefully, we could leave the ball-licking out of this week.

"What time is it?"

"We have fifteen minutes to meet the Jeep."

Agreeably, Alex rolled over and plodded to the bathroom. While he was distracted splashing water, I took the opportunity to unzip my backpack and slip out my camera. I had my favorite lens, the 250 mm, on, so I quickly pulled out my bigger zoom one, the 500 mm that I'd debated so hard about, and swapped them out. Just as I finished zipping up the backpack, Alex reemerged looking considerably more awake.

He slung a small bag over his shoulder. "Let's go."

Walking up to the main lodge building, we joined the rest of the guests in the open-air reception area. The roof was thatch, held together by glossy, dark natural logs, and the breeze sifted in, assisted by large, frond-shaped ceiling fans. The rest of the guests sat scattered around the room in brown leather chairs.

We must have been the last to arrive. As soon as we sat, a tall, Black woman, standing up at the front of the room, started the introduction.

"Amukela," she said, the name of the lodge. "This, in Zulu, means to receive or to welcome. On behalf of the staff, we are excited to have you here for the media tour."

Alex leaned toward me. "Media tour?"

I shushed him, keeping my eyes on her. She ran through the list of amenities available, social media accounts, hashtags, and then our daily schedule. It was the same thing every day for the week: our guides would take us out early in the morning, we'd be back in time for brunch, have a nap in the afternoon, and then another drive before a family-style dinner and bed.

Once we were dismissed, the drivers, who'd been standing in the corner waiting, called out names and divided us up into our Jeeps. There were a dozen of us split into three vehicles.

We greeted the couple joining us, Mark and Olivia, who ran a travel agency in America. Shortly, our driver, Thomas, called us to gather next to our Jeep. "And this is our tracker, Rex." A lean Black man in a pith hat and a staff uniform tipped his brim at us. "He also doubles as a barkeep, wait staff, and if the occasion calls for it, wrangler in the event of an animal situation." Thomas reached into the front seat of the vehicle and patted a rifle. "In case of an emergency while we are out on our drive, I'm prepared. Stick in the vehicle at all times, and you'll be fine. All right, let's load up."

The Jeeps had three rows: the front, where our driver sat, the middle, and the back. Alex and I climbed into the back seat, and to my astonishment, Rex sat not inside the Jeep but on a folding chair bolted to the front of the bonnet. We very quickly left the tiny patch of civilization and were in the wild. Bumps be damned, the scenery was gorgeous.

"There's been a family of wild dogs spotted the last few days over by one of the lakes," Thomas called out. "We're going to see if they're still there."

He wove us through the sand and shrubs, and I often had to lean away from the branches that thrust into the open-air Jeep as we passed. Rex, in his special seat, was unprotected but dodged with a practiced weave.

Sometimes, Thomas would slow down and shout out to Rex in one of the local languages. The sounds were soft and melodic, unlike the Germanic Afrikaans, so I guessed they spoke Xitsonga together. They'd converse for a minute, serious, before Thomas would give a chuckle and lurch us forward again.

After twenty minutes of driving, we emerged from the bushes to an open plain. The tire tracks in front of us were still clear, but Thomas paused us for a moment, and I watched as he and Rex scanned the surroundings.

We lurched again, up and over the hill, driving on toward a small lake. Rex pointed off in the distance, and Thomas whooped. "We got 'em!"

I squinted. Got what? As we approached, I realized the tiny dots of darkness in the golden grass were moving. As we closed on the animals, I could make out the lanky, lean figures, like mongrel dogs looking for tidbits off the street.

We slowed, and some of the dogs stopped to watch us. Thomas eased us to a stop and set the brake. He slung an arm over the empty passenger seat and faced us.

"These here are African wild dogs, a distant—very distant

—relation to domesticated dogs. There aren't that many of them in Kruger, so this is quite a treat."

I lifted my camera up, zooming completely in as far as I could. In profile, it looked just like a dog I'd see back home: panting, lolling tongue, canine teeth, and a black snoot. And then the dog turned its head, and I couldn't help but laugh. I pulled back as the Jeep crept forward.

"What?" Alex asked, a smile tugging his lips.

"Those ears! It looks like two satellite dishes on their heads!"

"We will get closer," Thomas assured us as the Jeep eased along. Heads turned towards us as the dogs watched, some of them standing, ears perked and guarded while we crept toward them. Their coats were covered in small spots of brown, black, and white, some blending in well with the brown and black of the landscape. I stifled a giggle again. As we got closer, all I could see was a field of round ears pointed at us.

I don't know what signal Thomas was waiting for, but I thought at any moment that the dogs would startle and run away. He kept inching forward and then finally stopped and set the brake.

For a moment, we all sat there in a standoff, waiting to see what would happen. I saw a shift of movement, a wriggle of hips, and put my camera up to my eye. Just in time, I caught the pounce. Two wild dogs tussled in the grass, another yawned. We were insignificant to them.

Our whole Jeep gasped and giggled as the dogs played. One went belly up in the dirt, kicking its heels up and lolling its tongue like a golden Labrador at the neighborhood dog park after a good soggy rain. Ears were chewed, tails were nipped, and my shutter—silent thanks to mirrorless DSLR technology—clicked away.

"Amazing." Alex's voice was breathless and surprisingly

close. I looked over my shoulder, and he had a pair of travel binos against his eyes, leaning toward my side of the vehicle. With his palm on the back of my seat, his body curved around me.

I watched his profile for a moment as his eyes moved around, his lashes sweeping against the eye cups and his mouth slightly open. His tongue came out and wet his lips, and my stomach tightened.

The binoculars dropped down, and Alex glanced over at me. "Sorry," he said, straightening up in his seat.

"It's okay. I'm glad you're enjoying it."

His lips curved up into a smile. "I am."

Our eyes held for just a moment before a gasp from Olivia snapped me out of it. I refocused on the dogs and tried not to wonder too hard if Alex was surrounding me again.

As the African wild dogs played, Thomas spoke quietly, telling us about the endangered species and the loss of their habitat, and the efforts to keep them away from livestock while still maintaining healthy packs in the park.

After ten minutes—and over a hundred photos—Thomas started the Jeep up again, and we lurched off. He took us along the edge of the lake, pointing out birds in flight and different plants on either side of us. A herd of zebras was off in the distance, too far off the track for us to approach, but he assured us they were common and we'd see plenty in our week-long stay.

The sky was starting to tinge darker, a warm filter settling over the land. We climbed up and over the hill, and the Jeep jerked to a halt. "Alright now, this is where we stop for a bit. You can get out and stretch your legs, but don't go too far. We'll have apps set up shortly."

Alex climbed down from the Jeep first, offering me a hand, but I gripped the door instead and hopped down. He put his hands in his pockets and shuffled behind me. Our hill was overlooking the lake, and I chided myself. I should have brought a tripod on the drive—rookie mistake. And a wide-angle lens wouldn't be remiss either.

But it was only our first drive. I would have a week of this, so for now, I'd take the best pictures I could.

I snapped photo after photo, wandering around and looking for anything interesting to stick in the foreground. Alex followed, always behind me, lifting the binos up to his eyes and taking it all in. For a few minutes, I was uncomfortable, wondering if he was watching me, but we moved around each other in silence, just enjoying our own view.

"Ladies and gentlemen," Thomas's voice cut into my thoughts, "drinks are served."

Mark and Olivia were still near and eagerly stepped up to the guides. Thomas and Rex had set up a cocktail hour; a small bar cart waited with a selection of drinks, and Rex stood behind it. Four wood and canvas chairs were set to look out over the lake, and a small table sat between each pair of chairs.

Alex brushed lightly past me as he headed toward the bar cart. "Gin and tonic, Nikki?"

My eyebrows raised. Alex remembered my favorite drink? "Please."

I kept snapping pictures, but Alex's voice carried over the gentle noises of the evening. He laughed easily with Rex while drinks were poured, and he clinked his glass with the two Americans when everyone had a drink.

Alex glanced up and caught me watching him. His smile turned smug, and I rolled my eyes before getting back to my camera. When I finally put the camera down and joined the group, Alex handed me my glass. I half expected a quip like, "It's not as good of a gin and tonic as I would make, you know I've taken a bartending study," or a challenge of, "Let's see who can correctly identify the botanicals in your gin." Instead, he tipped his glass to mine.

"Cheers, Nikki."

"Cheers."

As the cool bitterness slid down my throat, I thought this sounded like a truce.

FIVE

Upon returning from our drive, we were given thirty minutes to freshen up before dinner was served. The meal was amazing, the tables lit with candlelight and platters served family-style. Two roaring fireplaces on either side of the main lodge meant we didn't even notice the drop in temperature outside until we were trailing one of the guides back to our tent.

I followed Misola's footsteps and the bob of a lantern along the path as she spoke over her shoulder. "We sometimes get some wild animals here on the paths, but usually, if they hear you, they move away quickly."

I wrapped my arms around my waist, trying to keep warm, knowing we'd be back at the tent soon. Not that it would be any better there.

Alex trudged behind me. I was tired—exhausted—after a long day, and while I knew the cold was coming, it was sharper than I realized it would be. I was ready to curl up under the covers and sleep.

Despite his nap that afternoon, I doubted Alex was doing much better.

"Here you go." Misola raised the lamp ahead of us, and

the tent glowed softly from the lanterns through the canvas. The gauzy, light fabric, which had let in a breeze during the day, had been covered in roll-away canvas.

We thanked Misola and ducked through the flap of the tent. The room was warmly lit, with four lanterns spread throughout the space. It was even…romantic.

"Holy shit," Alex said behind me. "It's fucking freezing cold!"

I straightened up, never mind that I was cold and slightly miserable too. Tomorrow I'd bring a fleece to dinner for the walk back. "It *is* winter, Alex."

"Yes, well, I *do* know that. I just thought…well, it's Africa."

"Did you bring anything warm?"

"Not really, no."

We quickly took turns under the hot stream of water, and as soon as I slipped out of the bathroom, I leapt up onto the bed. I had on leggings and a long-sleeve cotton shirt, prepared for the cold. I was also pleasantly surprised to find a hot water bottle tucked inside the bed. I stretched a toe out and found one on Alex's side too.

The water shut off, and within moments Alex was hurriedly brushing his teeth, spitting into the sink, and leaping out of the bathroom too. I screeched when he launched himself over my side of the bed as he scrambled to get under the covers.

"Cold, cold, cold."

I blinked. Good lord. "What *are* you wearing?"

"Um. Boxers."

"You didn't pack pajamas?"

"One, I usually sleep naked, so I'm doing you a favor right now. Two, I didn't realize we'd be sharing a bed, as previously mentioned. Three, I was expecting it to be much warmer, and four, I also expected some kind of central air."

"Well," I said stiffly, "I'm sorry this vacation isn't living up to your standards. I don't know what you were prepared for, but these luxury safaris are—"

I was cut off by a sultry moan coming from Alex's side of the bed and some wobbling of the mattress that felt...scandalous. "What are you doing?" I raised up on my arm and glared at him. Pervert.

He cracked open an eye. "Did you know there are hot water bottles in the bed?"

I huffed and slouched back against the pillow. "Yes, I discovered that."

We were silent for a moment, the bed slightly shaking.

"Are you shivering?"

"I'll be fine."

I rolled my eyes and stared up at the ceiling. A ceiling I could see perfectly well, lit by all the lanterns. "Oh, for Pete's sake." I flipped the duvet open and darted around the room in my socks, turning each lantern off as quickly as possible and slipping back into bed.

We lay in the dark, the sounds of the bush surrounding us. It was odd to be this close to Alex—and a nearly naked Alex at that. I thought back to pool parties and teenaged Alex, shirtless and uncomfortable with his hormonal body, just like the rest of us.

But the concave chest was gone, replaced by a smooth and trim torso, and my brain stuttered a little when I replayed the curl of his body as he climbed into bed next to me.

I was sleeping next to Alex Boyd.

Bizarre.

―――――

My wake-up call was...unpleasant. In a series of moments, I was hit with the sounds of drums banging, the sensation of cold at the tip of my nose, and a heavy weight kicking me in the thigh.

"*Oof.*"

"Shite. Sorry, Nikki."

"What was that?"

"The drums to wake us up."

"No, not that," I said, exasperated in my morning fog. Er, it wasn't even morning. The tent was black, and it was impossible to tell the difference between when I fell asleep and when I woke up. Presumably, seven hours of sleep somehow had passed. "What was up with the David Beckham move?"

"I was just surprised...."

"Hello, morning, morning," a voice called from outside our flap.

Right. Wake-up calls and room service.

"Here are your beverages. Are you awake, Mr. and Mrs. Kozlova?"

"We're not the Kozlovas!" I shouted. "But yes! And thank you!"

With a click of a switch, the bedside light came on, and Alex's shoulders and lean body stood out in stark silhouette. His skin erupted in goose pimples when he escaped the confines of the warm bed.

"What are you going to wear for the morning drive?" I wondered.

He ran a hand down his face and back up into his hair. "I have no idea."

"I don't think you'll fit into my hiking pants. Do you want to try, anyway?"

I passed the clothing to him, and we turned away from each other, shivering as we quickly dressed.

"Well?"

Alex turned around, and my eyes were immediately drawn to the V of black briefs showing in the open zipper of my gray hiking pants.

"Good grief. That's a no." The pants wouldn't close over his hips. "Who knew you had such an arse, Alex."

"Look, I'll just wear my shorts."

I winced in sympathy. "The leggings I have are stretchy, but they will undoubtedly only go down to your knees. I'm afraid that's not going to do much."

He raised an eyebrow. "Still…"

———

FIFTEEN MINUTES LATER, WE EMERGED FROM THE TENT AFTER having gulped our hot teas down and polished off the morning biscuits even faster. Alex wore a pair of my leggings under his shorts, and, well…he looked ridiculous.

Who knew his thighs were so muscular?

A guide with a lamp was on the path and guided us in the dark to the Jeep.

"Right, climb on in. There's blankets and hot water bottles in the seats ready for you."

We launched ourselves in and piled the blankets over us, tucking in corners and wedging the hot water bottles in places where I never would have thought I would desire a water bottle.

Alex fidgeted next to me. "I think I should have taken off my boxers."

"You are NOT going commando in my leggings."

The drive was glorious. Rex had a big torch up front with him and swept patterns out ahead of us. We spotted all kinds of nocturnal wildlife before the sky started to brighten. Our truck lumbered up to a dry creek bed just as the sun peeked over the horizon, and, in the blissfully warmer air, we unloaded from the Jeep for a short walk.

Colorful birds flitted about in the morning, feasting on bugs. Rex pointed them out and gave us their names: bee-eaters, rollers, sunbirds.

Alex asked thoughtful questions about migration patterns and mating habits and conservation efforts while I clicked away with my camera. He was so engrossed in learning. I wondered if there would be a pop quiz later.

When we returned to the Jeep, Thomas had laid out a light breakfast of pastries and fruit. The four of us made plates and took our seats.

"How did you get into photography, Nikki?" Olivia asked.

"Yes," Alex swallowed his bite, "how *did* you get the photography bug?" His tone had a hint of humor in it like he knew I didn't want to answer.

Olivia looked at me expectantly, ready for some amusing anecdote.

I wilted. "I don't have a photography bug. I'm not very good at it."

"Oh, nonsense," Olivia waved a hand at me. "You wouldn't be here if you weren't good at it."

I cast about for something to say, anything other than talking about my camera. The last thing I wanted was to get Alex too interested in it.

"Did you know the African wild dogs regurgitate their food to feed their young like birds do?"

Olivia froze, the mini quiche halfway to her mouth.

"How fascinating," she said dryly.

Alex snorted.

———

I stepped through the entrance of our tent after returning from the drive and immediately froze.

Uh-oh.

Alex bumped into me from behind and put his hands on my shoulders to keep us from tumbling over. "What's wrong...oh."

Even standing behind me, Alex was tall enough to see the mess of our tent. Various items were scattered about: a tube of toothpaste here, a small glass bottle there, a smear of something creamy and beige over by the desk—on the concrete, thankfully.

"Did you put your toiletries in the trunk this morning?"

"Clearly not." When we'd been given the tour of our tent, our guide had told us to put things away in a locked trunk during the day to prevent curious monkeys from wrecking things. A reminder I clearly hadn't heeded well enough. "Fuck."

Alex squeezed around me into the tent, and I set myself in motion too. I grabbed a flannel from the washroom and wet it, wrung it out, and applied it to the big splotch of what was clearly my tinted moisturizer. Alex picked up items off the floor and tossed them on the bed.

"Well, they are very enterprising little buggers." He held up the torn toiletry bag from the far corner of the cabin. Something under the loveseat caught his eye, and he dropped to his knees to investigate. I huffed and went to the washroom to wring out the flannel.

"Uh, Nikki? Are you on medicine?"

I paused in wringing the cloth out. "Yeah. Antimalarials. Why?"

The curtain shifted, and Alex came in, holding a medicine pack that was clearly not my antimalarials. "I think you may have had a hand in reducing the monkey population by one or two monkeys."

I grabbed the pink disc from Alex. Yup, my birth control pills; all gone except for four of the seven placebo pills.

"There are still a few left," Alex said helpfully.

"Those are the placebos." I fiddled with the pack, running my finger over some bite marks in the packaging. "Thank you anyway."

Well, some monkey out there was going to have a weird menstrual cycle. And mine might go wacky for a bit. At least I wasn't dating anyone. There was no boyfriend to return to after a week away, and then have to explain that we'd have to use an alternative form of protection because a monkey had eaten my contraception.

"Right. Well." He shifted a step back. "I'll keep gathering your things."

When I stepped out of the washroom, there was a sizable pile of my toiletries on the bed. I ducked back in and grabbed the trash bin before plunking myself down and sorting the items out. The toothpaste was split, and Alex had had to clean minty-fresh paste off the carpet. Trash. Small vial of perfume with cap missing: keep, and possibly suffer from having too much perfume accidentally sprayed in my toiletry bag.

Alex went into the washroom and returned with the damp cloth. "What are you doing?" I asked.

"Well," he said, gesturing at the desk, a laugh escaping from his mouth. "One of the monkeys took great indignation with something and pissed on the desk."

"What? Oh my god." I put my hands to my mouth in horror. Those buggers. Thankfully, Alex was bent over laughing too hard to be horrified.

"I can clean it up," I offered.

"No, it's fine." He shooed me back to my pile of monkey food and chuckled as he turned to the puddle of piss. "Never let it be said I wouldn't do anything for you, Nikki."

SIX

DINNER WAS ANOTHER FABULOUS EVENING. ALEX AND I HAD SAT at one of the big family tables, drinking wine with four people from one of the other Jeeps: two brothers from Germany, Meino and Ernst, who ran a blog called *Two Traveling Bratwursts* and another couple from the States, Conrad and Rowena. Rowena wrote for freelance travel magazines. We laughed a lot, talking about travels and adventures. They were bubbly and enthusiastic, regaling us with stories of climbing Mount Kilimanjaro and what they hoped would be their next adventure: tickets on the SpaceX passenger flight.

"So," Conrad said, leaning back in his chair, "how long have you two been a couple?" His finger waggled between Alex and me.

"Oh, no. We aren't a couple," Alex clarified.

I let out a nervous chuckle. "No, no. We kissed once when we were teenagers, and Alex didn't like it very much. We are definitely not a couple."

"You didn't like it very much?" one of the German brothers asked. After two glasses of wine, I couldn't remember which brother was which. But the way this one's eyebrows rose and he looked Alex over, I could guess where his thoughts ran.

"Not like that," I chided. "Alex is straight."

The brother jabbed an invisible knife into his heart and groaned while Alex's ears turned strawberry.

"Sorry to disappoint, Ernst," Alex said, laughing.

Conrad's wife, Rowena, pulled me to the side as the conversation shifted.

"I noticed you have quite the camera with you."

I nodded. "Yes, it's an intense setup."

She dug into her bag. "I'm only carrying around this little camera. It's nothing as professional as yours." She pulled a small Nikon point-and-shoot camera out of her bag. "Would you be willing to take a look at my pictures? I think I screwed my settings up."

We flipped through her pictures on the screen, and I got acquainted with the buttons.

Rowena shook her head sadly. "This technology is just a bit beyond my skill set."

"Nonsense, don't discount yourself. You've been on some amazing adventures, and the important thing is the experience, right?"

She patted my arm. Rowena was in her sixties, if I had to guess, but very sprightly, as expected by a globe-trotter like her. "You're too young to understand just yet, but the memory's not what it used to be. And climbing Kili was nearly a decade ago. I didn't take enough pictures then, and I won't make the same mistakes now."

———

"What did you mean about the kissing thing?"

Alex leaned against the doorway to the toilet, the curtain fluttering by his side while I flossed back in our tent after dinner.

"I don't think it was a big mystery," I said between teeth, looking at him behind me via the mirror. "You didn't like it." I shrugged. "I'm over it. It was ages ago."

Alex watched me for a few moments before speaking up again. "I did like it."

I scoffed but kept my focus on my teeth, pulling the floss out and swallowing before answering. "Sure, you did. That's why you pushed me away, practically ran out the door, and told everyone I was a terrible kisser."

We had kissed at Tommy Mitchell's seventeenth birthday party. His parents hadn't been home, and like the rich kids you see in stereotypical Hollywood movies, he'd thrown a raging party. Unlike American movies, with keg stands and weed, the vices of choice had been X and the good scotch stolen from the liquor cabinet.

I hadn't done any drugs. But I had gone to hang out with Alex. After the graffiti incident, we'd had lunch every day and did our homework together. Alex tutored me in programming, and I helped him with maths.

But at the party, I'd been a horny, impatient seventeen-year-old with a whopping crush. And when Alex and I found each other alone in a hallway, I'd strapped on a pair and kissed him.

"Well," he said slowly, still watching me in the mirror, "I was a teenage boy no longer in control of his hormones, and the girl with the best tits in school had pressed them up against me. I had to run; otherwise, I'd have jizzed my pants."

My arms lowered, the floss unspooling from my fingertips on the way down until it dangled from my teeth.

When I didn't say anything, Alex tacked on, "Which part has got you tripped up? Jizzing in my pants or the spectacular tits bit?"

"Did you jizz your pants?"

"Nah. I made it to my car and came in the driver's seat. Dad still thinks the stain on the leather was mayonnaise."

I wrinkled my nose. "Ew."

He shrugged. "Teenage boy, great tits—and even better, they were attached to you."

My brain locked up for a moment, reprocessing the evening. The feel of Alex's lips on mine, being pushed away, my face burning. I came back to myself and finished flossing in a hurry. Alex still watched me, his arms folded across his chest.

I spit in the sink. "Then why did you tell everyone I was a terrible kisser?"

He rubbed his chin. "Now, about that part. Either we have different recollections, or something got bungled. Because I seem to recall you said *I* was a terrible kisser."

"Who told you that?"

"Bernice. Who told you I said you were a terrible kisser?"

"Bernice." I narrowed my eyes. Bernice, one of my former friends who Alex dated for all of Year Twelve.

"Well, didn't that work out nicely for her then?" I tossed the floss in the bin under the sink and banged around for a bit, putting Alex's toothpaste on my brush and aggressively attacking the plaque on my teeth.

Over my furious brushing, Alex continued. "Here's the thing. We probably *were* rubbish."

"Speak for yourself," I grumbled around the toothbrush.

"We were seventeen, Nikki."

I kept my eyes straight ahead. Talking about kissing Alex with Alex was irritating me.

"I think I've gotten a lot better at it," he went on. "I wouldn't have known what to do with you back then. You were confident, and I was fumbling around. I would have wanted it to be good. I would have wanted to please you."

My brushing slowed, and my eyes found his in the mirror.

"I would have wanted to take my time. I would have wanted a better first kiss than one in the hallway around our high friends. I would have wanted to go slow and learn every possible noise that I could pull out of you. Seventeen-year-old me wouldn't have been able to do that."

Alex's eyes burned through me. My stomach flipped. He waited a beat and then heaved himself off the wall. "Let me know when you're done in there," he called over his shoulder.

I watched him leave in the mirror and then caught my own reflection. The toothbrush dangled from my mouth, a bit of foam dripping out from my lip.

I looked rabid.

I felt rabid.

———

I LAY IN BED LISTENING TO THE SOUNDS OF ALEX GETTING READY to sleep. *Seventeen-year-old me wouldn't have been able to do that.*

Holy shit.

I curled up on my side, facing away from Alex's side of the bed. I was…horny. My muscles involuntarily contracted and clenched my thighs together. Those words kept playing in my head over and over again.

I hated to admit it, but Alex was right. Seventeen-year-old Alex and seventeen-year-old Nikki would have bungled things. It was all too easy to think about the sexual experiences I had in secondary school and uni; I didn't know what I was doing, and most of the boys I'd been with hadn't known either.

Not that I'd particularly had any amazing experiences since then. I had often wondered if I should date outside of my social circle, try to find someone who was older and knew what they were doing. Ion had been my longest relationship, and it had fizzled out of the hot-and-heavy stages very quickly.

And aside from a flurry of one-night stands after our

breakup, I hadn't been seeing anyone, too focused on this new career path to have time to date.

The light switch clicked off in the bathroom, and I clenched my eyes shut. Maybe I could feign sleep. I needed time to mull over those words.

Alex darted around the bed, flopping in quickly and tugging the covers toward himself to escape the cold. Another click and the light was out.

The bed quivered as Alex adjusted himself—not *himself* as in his dick, I hoped—and we settled into silence.

I stared off into space.

Alex was *right* there. Grown-up, twenty-five-year-old Alex was sharing a bed with me, possibly in just a T-shirt and boxers, all warm and smooth skin and…

My thighs clenched again.

It was going to be a long night.

SEVEN

Our Jeep slowed, and Thomas picked up the radio and chattered at someone in Afrikaans while the vehicle rolled to a stop. Next to me, Alex leaned in towards the center and glanced around. We were on a dusty path following along a dry riverbed in the mid-morning. I tried to imagine what this place would look like in the wet season with leaves budding on the trees and the sounds of rushing water filling the air. Today, where we were, seemed unusually still.

Our morning had been weird. It had begun with him startling me awake *again* as the drums went off. We dressed and ate quietly, shivering with more than just the cold hanging over us. I'd caught glimpses of him in my leggings before he slipped his shorts on over them, but this time it hadn't been quite as funny.

...every noise I could pull out of you.

I could easily imagine myself hearing those words every morning for the rest of my life. Those were the kind of words that hung around.

An awkwardness lurked over us. Those words echoed, and the intimacy of the tent changed our relationship.

We'd kept our distance in the back of the Jeep, Alex quiet and bundled up. Did he regret his honesty? I had abandoned my camera in my lap, the strap around my neck, so I could tuck my hands in and keep warm as we'd left the compound. Now, in the mid-morning air, it was tepid, and the sun was beating down.

"Okay," Thomas said, twisting in his seat to look at us. "There's a report of a lion kill by one of the watering holes. We have just enough time to make it out there, and if we find them quickly, watch for a little while. The other Jeeps are too far away to make it back before breakfast, so we might have it all to ourselves. Just a reminder, it is very important to stay seated while we are near the big cats, yeah?"

A chorus of agreement sounded as Thomas fired up the engine again. Mark and Olivia chatted excitedly in the seats in front of us. Alex and I exchanged a glance, giving each other small, excited smiles as the eagerness eased some of the tension.

We traveled for fifteen minutes, gripping the handles as the Jeep lurched over rocky terrain or made a sharp turn. Thomas must be really worried about making it back in time; he was hauling ass.

We paused at the crest of a hill, and Rex gave a hand signal as Thomas eased us down.

"Nikki," Alex said, nudging me and pointing off into the distance. There was a splash of dark against the tan ground and some movement.

We grew closer, and I could make out the shapes now. The largest lump was a giraffe, legs akimbo and stomach torn open. I grimaced as we drew closer.

The truck slowed to a stop. I glanced ahead, and the road curved off and to the right, meaning this was as close as we would get to the lions.

They were on Alex's side, not mine, and my view was blocked by the seat in front of him.

I faffed about, looking for a better angle with my camera. I just couldn't see it from my seat. I must have let out a noise, and Alex dropped his binos. "Come on." He gestured me closer.

I scooted along the seat until our thighs pressed together. Yes, okay, now I could see. I leaned slightly over Alex, ducking underneath his arms, which were back to holding up the binos.

Steading my camera with both hands, I zoomed in. Overwhelmed, I fidgeted around for a moment, looking at each of the big cats. Vaguely I heard Thomas tell us there were four females here and two nearly grown males that would be forced out of the pack soon.

There was always at least one with an eye on us, observant and protective. I snapped shot after shot, even having to zoom out a bit to capture more of the surroundings. But with this lens, my 500 mm, I could zoom in completely, and my vision would be filled with teeth and blood and offal. It was gruesome and spectacular.

My arms were growing too tired, and I wanted to get a bit lower—just a smidge—to take more shots. I nestled my elbow onto the seat, between the side of the Jeep and Alex's leg. I vaguely felt my foot lift off the floorboard and carefully maneuvered my leg around the backpack.

One of the lionesses yawned, a great gaping maw of teeth. I snapped away, catching a lolling tongue, a quiver of whiskers.

Now my foot was pressing against the opposite wall of the Jeep, and I stretched lightly, working myself into a more comfortable position. I wasn't leaning out the Jeep, but I had definitely wiggled my way into a better angle.

I snapped again and again. "Come on, you beautiful girl," I whispered, "give me your other side."

I waited patiently, zooming out to see the group and keeping an eye on the whole scene. I kept clicking. I could have filled my card and probably not gotten enough pictures of the lions.

But after a few minutes, the truck rumbled to life underneath me.

"Time to head back to camp," Thomas called out. "Everyone ready?"

I grudgingly agreed, and the rest of the group echoed reluctantly around me. Alex was quiet.

As Thomas pulled us out, I pulled my face away from the viewfinder and fiddled with the buttons. God, I hoped some of those photos came out. I flipped through a few before I glanced out the side again and spotted Alex's hand clenched on the rail next to my head. His knuckles were white, and I glanced up at his face as we bounced along. His jaw was tense, eyes staring straight ahead.

Right. I was spread out over his thighs like a masochist looking for a spanking from Daddy. My boobs were in his lap, jostling about with the bumpy ride. The one saving grace was that I wasn't actually boob-first on his cock; instead, maybe, *maybe*, his cock was boob-adjacent.

I braced myself against the side rail and lurched upward, scrambling to get out of this position, dignity completely out of the question. Unfortunately, I didn't take into account the location of Alex's face.

I got a whack on the back of my head and let out a little cry, but it was covered by Alex's echoing, "Fuck!"

He grabbed his face, and the Jeep slowed.

"Everything okay back there?" Thomas called out, just as a trickle of blood slipped beneath Alex's fingers.

"No, Alex is bleeding!" I shouted back at him.

Thomas braked to a stop as I fumbled around in my backpack for a tissue or serviette or anything I could use to stop the blood. I pulled out the closest thing I had, a spare lens cloth. Not very absorbent, but it was something. I unwrapped it from the plastic.

"Here," I said as I held it up to Alex's face. He pulled his hand back, and I swooped in with the cloth. Goodness, that was bloody.

"Alex, I'm so sorry."

The car door popped open next to us, and Thomas's face appeared etched with concern. "The good news is, we're far enough away from the lions," he joked. "And you aren't nearly as appetizing as the giraffe, even if you smell like blood."

The lens cloth was absolute rubbish for sopping up a wet mess, but in a quick moment, Thomas had a medical cotton out and was gently nudging my hand out of the way.

Alex was eased down from the car, and Mark, who was a doctor back in the States, checked him over while Thomas and Rex dug out water bottles from the boot. Blood mopped up and washed away into the dirt, we cleaned Alex up as best we could. My leggings would need a good hand washing in the sink when we returned to the lodge.

We climbed back into the vehicle again, Alex with cotton inelegantly stuffed up his nostrils.

"I really am sorry," I said sincerely. I felt my apology had gotten lost in the mayhem, and Alex hadn't said a word to me. Not since I'd forced my tits onto him and not even when I'd caused him to leak irresistible blood that surely wafted across the savanna to every predator within miles. Good thing the closest ones were satiated.

"It's fine," Alex said, finally looking at me.

"But I made you bleed."

"You also did me a favor." He shifted in his seat.

"I did?"

Alex leaned in close to me, and despite the dried blood and sexy nostril plugs, I leaned toward him.

"It's hard to keep a boner when you're bleeding."

I turned away quickly to hide a smile, my cheeks heating up as Alex's laughter rang out.

EIGHT

THAT AFTERNOON OUR DRIVE WAS A LITTLE DIFFERENT. RATHER than each Jeep splitting up and heading into the wilderness in search of animals, we were all visiting one of the local villages.

Thomas explained, "This land is all part of the tribe's remittance. And the lodge partners with the locals to share the profits and to promote the education of the people. Amukela has sent two dozen locals on scholarship to become certified rangers, and many more work in the service side of the lodge or get English and hospitality lessons. In exchange, the people want you to come and see their way of life."

"Are you from here?" Meino asked.

"No, I am from Botswana. But I've been here for many years, and on my off time, I stay in the village."

"Are cameras okay?" I asked.

Thomas nodded. "Yes, the village wants people to explore and share their culture. Photographs are fine."

He fielded a few other questions, and then we gathered into the Jeeps.

We drove along the road rather than the dusty trails in the park, still seeing wildlife here and there; elephants rumbling through the trees or giraffe heads poking above the treetops. Thomas always pointed them out, but we didn't stop.

We slowed as we approached a fence constructed with large, rough-hewn posts pressed tightly together. Over the wood, I could just barely make out the thatched rooftops of a few buildings. The Jeep rolled to a stop next to a rusted lorry and a few motorbikes.

Thomas shouted out as we walked through the opening in the fence, and he was greeted by loud calls back. The village was set up with different stations, and there were adults seated on the ground with blankets spread out in front of them, and Thomas led us to the first one. A tall man with peppered gray hair and a short beard stood behind it wearing a loincloth and holding a spear. All of the villagers were similarly dressed, women in fur skirts and men in loincloths. All the adults were bare-chested, and I worried my lip. I wanted to photograph the experience but also wanted to be respectful of their culture and bodies. The man stared at us, sternly, and I began to wonder if we weren't as welcome here as Thomas made it sound.

But then the man cracked the largest smile I'd ever seen. He said something to us that I couldn't understand but then switched to English.

"That means welcome in Xitsonga. I am Kuhlula, and this is my village. Thank you for joining us." His English was halted and careful. "Please, sit."

He gestured down at the dirt, and I folded my legs under me as I sat. The eight of us formed a circle around Kuhlula's mat, which was filled with clippings of plants and flowers. Picking up a bouquet of slender stems with purple flowers, he handed them out. "This morning, I walked for you. I will show you how to survive in the savanna, just in case Thomas loses you." His eyes twinkled.

Kuhlula guided us through all the plants in front of him, teaching us which ones held water, which ones could be used for practical purposes, like an antiseptic, and which ones were poisonous. We nibbled on plants that didn't taste very good, but if you had to choose between eating them and starving, at least you'd know.

It could be a tough life out there.

We went from blanket to blanket, sitting and learning some aspect of the tribe's life. Kuhlula often stood to the side and spoke for his villagers. The last blanket was full of handicrafts for sale. "Please explore our village. If you want to make a weaving or try on a piece of jewelry...." Kuhlula made an open gesture with his hand.

The two German brothers made a beeline for the men carving tools and weapons. They didn't hunt in this traditional way much anymore, though they kept up sports for their heritage. Alex, to my surprise, wandered over to the kids who played under the watchful eye of a matronly woman sitting in the shade of the fence. The wide-eyed children approached him, and he squatted down to talk. I held the camera up to my face and snapped some photos as Alex chatted with them. The kids all knew English pretty well; as Kuhlula had explained, it was now compulsory in school. Alex and the young girl, maybe eight years old, started holding up fingers and counting together in Xitsonga. She giggled at his pronunciation, repeating words back to him until he got it right. Soon they were surrounded by the rest of the kids, and Alex had them teaching him songs.

Someone tugged on my sleeve, a child—four years old? — with wide eyes and a snotty nose. He pointed at the screen of my camera.

"You are a smart little tot, aren't you?" I crouched down further and aimed the camera his way. I snapped a few shots and pointed the screen toward us. He saw his own face on the camera and squealed in delight.

Of course, that drew attention, and soon all the kids were around me, posing for pictures and mugging for the camera. I took shot after shot, delighting them until Thomas rounded the guests up, and we loaded back into the Jeep. Many of the villagers came out to wave goodbye as we pulled away, waving back.

———

As we cleaned up for dinner, Alex asked me if I had enjoyed the village visit.

"I did. You seemed to make friends pretty easily with the kiddos."

"So did you," he pointed out from the bathroom. "I've never been to a place like that."

"What do you mean?" I asked while I cleaned and checked my camera gear.

"We didn't travel much when I was a kid, with Mum always working. If we did, it was just around the continent, not really exploring cultures beyond our own. With the exception of going back to Malaysia to visit some of Mum's family."

"What is that like?"

"Ah, we don't do anything touristy there. I guess it's culture by proxy; we get to see what life is like for Mum's family, the everyday quiet type of life. What about you? Have you been to villages like that before?"

I shook my head, even though he couldn't see me. "No, most of my trips have been in the Mediterranean."

"Didn't you go to the Maldives last year?"

Alex had a good memory of Ion's Instagram, which seemed so weird since he pretty much hated Ion. Why keep following Ion when he didn't even like him? What was he looking for?

And then I thought of every time Alex told me Ion wasn't right for me. Every time he called him Party Boy. Every time he said we had nothing in common.

And that last time, when he asked me if I really thought Ion was the one.

What had Alex seen? What had he known about me?

I mentally shook myself, returning to Alex's question. "Yes, but it was an all-inclusive resort, and it's very segregated there. Most of the staff was Maldivian, but they all spoke English and had hospitality training. It's big business over there. I regret not going to a village."

"Well, it looked like you got plenty of sun and swim while you were there."

I didn't know what to say to that. Ion's feed had pictures of me, too: in a bikini off the deck of the overwater bungalow, kisses at sunset, cocktails by the pool.

Alex came out of the bathroom, drying his hands. "What about Russia?"

I shook my head again. "Never been, not since we moved, anyway."

Alex sat on the bed to affix his watch back on his wrist. "What is that about? Was your dad in the Russian mob or something?"

"If I told you, I'd have to kill you." I zipped up my bag and started toeing on my flats.

Alex looked me up and down. "Mmm." He rubbed his chin while his eyes dropped down low again. "Very Bond Girl of you."

I aimed a finger gun at him. "Come on, I'm ready for a drink."

Alex shook his head. "I'm going to stay behind for a bit and shave." He ran his fingers over his cheek. "I'm getting a bit itchy."

Alex had grown a little bit of scruff around the edges of his jawline. It occurred to me that traveling with Alex was affording me an odd privilege. I had never seen Alex anything less than cleanly shaven. "Oh, all right."

"I'll meet you at the bar." Alex mock-saluted before returning to the bathroom.

I ducked out of the tent. In my mind, I could see Alex leaning over a steamy sink, the mirror slightly fogged up, and his face lathered with shaving cream.

Shirtless, of course.

I made it ten paces up the path before stopping. My brain was having a really filthy fantasy, and I was too busy trying to fill the gaps to even bother walking. Would he be wearing a towel or his shorts? What would his shaving cream smell like? What kind of razor did he use?

I bit my lip.

The files from the day's safari *did* need to be transferred over to my laptop. I could get that set up, and then, maybe, we would be able to walk together to dinner. The files would transfer while we ate and be done when we returned.

The opportunity for a further peek into Alex's world was too much for me to pass up.

I backtracked and unzipped the gauzy entrance to the tent again. Toeing off my shoes, I peered around, hoping to catch Alex at the sink.

Rather, the space in front of the sink was empty, and I pinched my eyebrows together, wondering where Alex had gone.

Out of sight, water turned on, the hot water heater clicking over and the pounding of the shower hitting the tile. Alex hadn't closed the curtain. I'd assumed he was shaving at the sink, but instead, he was in the shower. I barely saw a flash of skin before I ducked out of the shower block. My cheeks flushed, and I berated myself. What was I trying to accomplish here?

And then Alex started humming a delightful rendition of Toto's "Africa," and I suppressed a giggle.

———

AFTER DINNER, WE MADE OUR WAY BACK TO THE TENT. THE manager had pulled me aside and asked if I still wanted time to do a photo shoot the next day, and I had said yes. Getting to take pictures while everyone else was gone would be really helpful—both to me and the lodge—so I wanted to stay behind from the drive.

But I also needed to do it without Alex in my way.

It took me until we were both in bed with the lights out to finally say something. "I'm not going on the drives tomorrow," I said into the blackness.

The bed bounced as Alex sat up. "Hang on a minute." He switched on the lamp beside him. "You just *aren't going* on the drive tomorrow?"

"I have some things I have to do tomorrow."

"Well, then I'll stay behind with you. Take a pool day, yeah?"

"You're still going on the drive tomorrow," I said. "I'd like some privacy."

"Privacy?"

When I looked at Alex, I thought I'd see anger. Instead, his brow was creased, a frown tipping his lips down.

"I thought we were getting on better," he said. "You know, we haven't really fought, and it's been...what? Thirty-six hours?"

"And let's keep it that way. Give me a day off."

His frown deepened, his eyes narrowing. "Fine," he bit out, rolling back to turn the lamp off.

———

ONE WOULD THINK AFTER AN EXCITING FEW DAYS OF EARLY wake-up calls in the morning, wildlife sightings all day, and long social dinners, I would have enjoyed a lovely lie-in on my morning off from the drive.

Given that I needed daylight to take my pictures, I had

expected to sleep in while Alex crept out. But I was woken up again by Alex jerking in bed at the drums, nearly knocking me off the mattress. He was extra loud getting dressed and ready to leave, presumably payback for telling him I needed some time alone.

At least I'd gotten to watch him pull on the leggings over his underwear. Usually, I was too busy dressing or using the toilet.

When he finally unzipped the entrance to our tent and left, I should have slipped right back into dreamland. Instead, I tossed around a bit, unmoored. Yes, I was disappointed to be sitting out the drive, but I was here in my capacity as a photographer, and I was excited and nervous to spend the whole day on a photo shoot.

That was all this was, right?

It had nothing to do with not getting to spend the day with Alex again. It was certainly easy to slip back into friendship with him, but I had to remember that he was wily.

Right. I tried to focus my thoughts. He used to be so passive-aggressive on Ion's Instagram, always making comments with an undertone of snark.

And I thought back to Alex waiting for me at the finish line of the London Marathon, looking smug and startlingly refreshing, as if forty-two kilometers had been nothing for him.

He'd been shirtless, his hair a little long at the time, slicked back with sweat and the dampness that was October in London. Unlike most of the male runners, Alex wasn't lean anymore. His height, for a while, had surpassed his muscles, and he'd been a gangly teen. But adult Alex, while still lean, had been surprisingly muscled.

I think it was the first time I'd seen Alex without a shirt on as an adult. Long gone were the pool parties of our youth.

Focus back on the smug face, Nikki.

Right, smug and confident, knowing that not only had he

had more money pledged than me, but he also roundly beat my time.

I curled up on my side a bit more. Without Alex in bed with me, the temperature was dropping fast. I tugged the blankets toward me from either side to tuck myself in tighter. A hand with a mind of its own wandered over to Alex's side of the bed. It was still warm, but maybe that was just my imagination.

I flopped over face first, checking with my cold nose. No, definitely not warm anymore. Mmm…but it smelled good.

We were four nights into this crazy trip, and sharing a bed with Alex hadn't been awful. No, my accidental titty-fuck while watching lions feast was the stuff of dark porn, but that had been the worst of it.

And he'd been surprisingly kind about it, making me laugh rather than teasing me.

The sheets smelled like Alex, reminding me a bit of the ocean. I breathed in deeper, trying to memorize the scent.

There's something to be said for pheromones. A few wayward thoughts about Alex's chest and a few whiffs of his bed, and I was clenching my legs together again. Well, I supposed it helped that my sex life had been remarkably unsatisfying too.

I squirmed on the bed, twisting my hand under my shirt and into my pants. It was easy to close my eyes, to remember the way his body felt when we'd been pressed up together in the Jeep. I thought about the way he said my name in the mornings, voice still gritty from sleep.

Dipping my fingers in, feeling how slick I was, I tried to imagine the parts of him I didn't know. What if we'd had that first kiss, not in the hallway of a loud party, but in one of those quiet moments we'd had at my house? I hadn't been brave enough to kiss him when we were alone, and teenaged me somehow thought a party was better.

Kids are idiots.

What if we had kissed in private? What if we kissed here? I used to think Alex didn't respect me, didn't think I was good at anything. I wasn't so sure anymore.

I moved up to my clit, pressing harder, giving myself the force I needed to see stars. If I made a move here in this bed later tonight, would he pull away? Or would I have his lean hips between my thighs, his drive and ambition turned into something that would be unlike anything I had ever experienced?

After only a few minutes of touching myself, I came hard, clamping around my hand, gasping into the still-dark canopy of our bed.

Alex could turn anything into a competition. Which suddenly didn't sound so bad.

NINE

THE EXCITED CHATTER OF THE GUESTS COMING IN OFF OF THE JEEP interrupted my conversation with Delina, the bartender. It was nearly time for brunch, and I'd been smelling the meal for the past hour during my kitchen photo shoot. I had clicked away while the team of chefs prepared the food, and my memory card was full of swirling steam, crisp, fresh produce, and the laughing faces of the staff. Like the guides, most of them were locals, but unlike the guides with impeccable English, most of the kitchen and service staff spoke Xitsonga around me.

I had eaten a little—bites here and there. On one of my earlier shoots, the one with Ion in the Maldives, I'd learned the fastest way to build camaraderie with the staff, and to make them comfortable in front of the camera, was to be an overexaggerated version of myself. Especially when, like now, the staff didn't always speak English. The kitchen staff was the way in with the rest of the staff—a few yummy noises and eye rolls of pleasure, and Bob's your uncle. You'd get delicious food, and people would relax.

I didn't have to fake it, either. The food was amazing. We'd dined on kudu steaks and traditional Cape Malay curries, a reflection of the diverse faces of the kitchen staff. Today's brunch meal was bobotie, a dish similar to shepherd's pie but made with egg custard on top rather than potatoes and heavily laden with curry spices.

The bar was swarmed by the incoming guests, and I took my glass of water and grabbed a seat at the table. I inspected the serving bowls in front of me. Odd. One held sliced bananas, another raisins, and another flaked coconut. What in the world were we eating? What happened to the bobotie?

Alex straddled the bench next to me. "I thought you should know what you missed out on today."

I raised an eyebrow at him. "Oh?"

"Cheetahs. A family of them rolling in the sand and playing together." Alex's smug face was back, and I nearly rolled my eyes. *Look, I can safari better than you can.*

I was saved a snarky comment by Olivia sitting down and chiming in across from me. She leaned across the table and offered me a look at her photographs. "Nothing as good as you would have done," she said demurely.

After flipping through the photos and oohing and aahing —she had done a remarkable job—we were interrupted by one of the wait staff setting down the bobotie, deep steaming platters that were filled to the brim with a crisp, crackling top shell of egg.

"This is bobotie," our server, whose name tag read Sam, said, "one of South Africa's most popular dishes." She gripped the serving spoon and scooped out a hearty portion of the dish, leaving heavily spiced steam wafting upward. She then showed us the condiments, the fruits I had noticed earlier, and a tangy and sweet chutney. "That is how South Africans eat it."

We dug in, piling the banana, raisins, and coconut on our plates and experimenting with the odd mix of flavors and textures. It was shockingly good, though unusual.

"Will you be joining us this afternoon, Nikki?" Olivia asked me.

"No, unfortunately. I'll be here waiting to join for dinner, though."

Olivia glanced at Alex and then smiled at me. "Don't worry, we'll make sure Alex isn't too lonely back there."

Between mouthfuls of food, Alex gave her a charming smile. "You are delightful company, Olivia."

She tittered. Such a charmer.

My afternoon agenda was more photo shoots of the guest rooms, the pool, and cocktails that Delina whipped up. And, helpfully, Sam had offered to assist me in some staged shots around the grounds at sunset.

But first, it was nap time for everyone, and the staff was going to be busy cleaning the lodge. Once our plates were empty, the guests began filtering back to their tents. I followed behind Alex, buoyant and energetic. It was remarkable how much the safaris wore you out, I thought, as Alex yawned in front of me.

He slipped into the bathroom for the post-safari scrubbing of sand and sunscreen, and I pulled out my laptop to transfer files, switched SD cards, and cleaned my lens. I wasn't tired, but Alex was surely going to nap.

Sure enough, when I stepped out of the bathroom, Alex was in bed, having kicked off the heavy duvet and lying sprawled under the light sheet.

I settled at my laptop to check up on the files. I moved files around, named some folders, clicked a few things here and there.

"Nikki," came a sharp voice.

I looked up to Alex glaring at me. "What?"

"Your keyboard is very loud."

"You're a light sleeper." *Great insult, Nikki.*

He grunted and glared some more before flopping over.

I sighed and closed my laptop. The files were transferring. I really could leave it be.

Instead, I picked up my e-reader and climbed into bed on my side. Alex grunted again.

"Hush, I'm getting settled, and I'll be super quiet, I promise."

I curled up on my side, my e-reader in hand, and settled into my book. Then I felt a twitch on the bed. And then again.

Oh my god, Alex was out like a light already. He may be a light sleeper, but he fell asleep quickly.

I read a few pages of my book, and then Alex shifted on the bed behind me. I almost jerked as an arm snaked its way around my waist, a warmth pressing against my back. The straps of my tank top barely covered my upper back, and Alex's bare skin pressed against me.

Who knew Alex was a cuddler?

I stifled a chuckle and kept reading, Alex's breath warm and heavy on the back of my neck. It was funny at first, but then it shifted. He was heavy and comfortable, and I wanted to snuggle myself in closer.

But Alex was a light sleeper, and I stayed still for fear of waking him up and having to face his ire again.

I did, however, keep an eye on the time, and as the clock ticked toward the hour, I braced myself for the banging of drums and the ensuing flailing.

Alex did not disappoint. The drums pounded, and Alex sharply inhaled over my shoulder and immediately jerked into action. Since I was braced this time, Alex's momentum carried him sailing off his side of the bed.

I couldn't have hoped for better.

I shoved my face into my pillow to try to muffle my laughter, but that was a worthless endeavor. I turned my head and watched Alex rise, bleary through my tears. His face was flushed, jaw gritted.

Wiping tears from my eyes, I sat up. "Alex," I gasped out,

trying for mock horror and failing horribly. "You are a cuddler!"

He brusquely wrenched the sheets up to the top of the bed, quite unnecessarily, since our bed was made every afternoon while we were out on safari. "I am not."

The apparent indignity against my proclamation made me laugh harder, and Alex stomped off to use the facilities. He said nothing to me as he gathered his things.

"Oh, Alex, come on. Don't be a grump. I'm just teasing."

He stopped just inside the flap of the tent. "Did you like it?"

My laughter died. "Did I like what?"

"Did you like it when I cuddled you?" he asked. The graveness of the question swept the humor out of the room like a chilling breeze.

I swallowed hard.

"Maybe," he said, just before ducking out the door, "that's why you need some time away from me."

TEN

"Hold the drink a bit higher," called Sam. I lifted the bee's knees cocktail up and hoped she knew what she was talking about. I had the camera set up on a tripod, the framing down to a tee, so I supposed her feedback was better than her trying to adjust the camera.

It was odd to sit for my own camera with someone else in control. Sometimes I set it up for myself with a remote clicker to trigger the shutter, but more often, I was the one behind the lens. Or at least I had been with Ion.

"Okay, I think we got it."

I put the cocktail down and sauntered over to the camera. I looked through the photos and breathed a sigh of relief. They were perfect. Daylight was fading, and we were losing the light, but this photo was exactly what I had in mind. I was facing away from the camera, my wide-brimmed hat making me unrecognizable as I looked out toward the colorful sky, a cocktail in hand and oil torches lighting the deck around me.

Just perfect.

"Sam, this is fabulous. You are doing such a great job." She ducked her head, and we both grinned. "Okay, last one.

To the bar!" I pointed skyward in a tally-ho gesture, and we laughed.

"That is where everyone wants to be," she confirmed.

We set up the last shot, ditching the hat in exchange for turning my head away from the camera. This time I set up the framing and tripod to accentuate my slinky dress and heels. The dress was bright red, full of curves. The pose with the cocktail on the deck overlooking the sunset had only shown my shoulders and straps. This one was a full-length shot.

The bar was candle-lit, the roaring fire going, and there was just enough light to barely pull this off. It was dark and sexy and luxurious.

I struck my pose, and Sam snapped away, giving me gentle directions while I held a martini. I kept reminding myself to relax my shoulders, fix my posture, suck in my tummy, all the little things a model knows to do to make the photo better.

Ion had been much better at this than me. But I was learning.

"What is this?" Alex's voice rang out through the hall. I'd been so focused I hadn't noticed the distant chatter of the guests approaching from the lot.

Without moving, I called out to him, "Hang on, we're almost done. Right, Sam?"

"Yeah. Maybe…look down a bit more?"

I tilted my head, and after a pause, she called it. I broke my pose, checked the shots, and thanked her again.

"No worries. It's good timing. I'll get back to the kitchen now."

That left Alex and me alone. The rest of the guests must have been dropping their gear off, freshening up for dinner.

"What were you doing?"

I looked Alex up and down; his fist gripped the strap of his binos, turning the knuckles white. In the growing darkness, I couldn't make out the brown of his irises.

"Sam was helping me take photos."

"For what?"

I shrugged while packing up my things, setting my lenses carefully in the backpack.

"Let me guess, Ion got you doing your own Instagram thing now?"

That gave me pause. It was partially true—I did have my own Instagram account that I used to promote my travels and my sponsored trips like this one. But it was also anonymous—hence the large hats and head-turning.

Alex had been so derisive of Ion's Instagram account. Which, yes, I did understand that for most people, an Instagram account is a rather frivolous thing. But Alex didn't know the behind-the-scenes of it; he'd never bothered to ask or think about what went into Ion's social media and how much it impacted his career.

Or the thought of who was behind the lens taking those pictures. Ion's Instagram account, and his career, had been languishing when I took over for him. And look where his career had climbed.

"Yes, it's for Instagram," I said, imbuing my voice with as much haughtiness as I could. "So what?"

Alex said nothing, but the tick in his jaw gave him away. And I couldn't help it. "My followers are going to *love* that shot. I mean, it just screams *Out of Africa* meets James Bond heroine. Just look at this dress." I waved my hand down my body, looking down at myself. When I looked up, Alex had followed my instructions precisely. His gaze traveled down my legs to the tips of my toes. I watched in silence as they roamed back up, intense, as if looking through the dress and seeing the thong I'd packed just for this session.

No panty lines here.

When his eyes locked on mine, I shuddered. That was a very dangerous look, and I was angry with him. I zipped up the backpack with force and slung it over my shoulder. "Now, if you'll pardon me, I need to go clean up and change for dinner."

I passed him in a huff, and the click-click of my heels was followed by the soft squeak of Alex's sneakers.

"Where are you going?" I turned around, and Alex came to an abrupt stop.

"To clean up," he said, lifting both arms from his side and dropping them back down. "I was the one who got dirty today out in the wild. You'd be right at home for cocktails in that dress." He arched an eyebrow at me.

"Fine." I turned before I rolled my eyes and continued out of the main building. The way back to the tent was a boardwalk, and I carefully placed my steps on the boards so as to not hook a heel between the slats.

I was very aware of Alex behind me, thrumming with impatience. We finally made it to the tent, where the flaps were down and the lanterns lit, giving the room a soft glow. It was nearly dark now, and the temperature was dropping. I needed to change into something much warmer.

"Why are you doing the Instagram thing?" Alex asked, leaning against the bed rather than making use of the facilities to get ready for dinner.

"It's fun, and I enjoy it. Is that so wrong?" I challenged.

"Of all the things you do, why did you stick with that one? You are always so flighty; why not now?"

Seriously? I'm flighty? My anger boiled over. "What is your problem? You've always been a jerk about Instagram, and I don't understand it. It doesn't do any harm, so just leave it be. Stop hating on Instagram."

"I don't hate Instagram. I am on it, after all." Alex crossed his arms, his voice raising to match mine.

"Ah, yes, I remember the first time you commented on one of Ion's posts. You said, 'Looks like someone's having fun.'" I put it in mocking air quotes with my fingers. "Could you have been more condescending?" It was a photo of Ion doing shots with some of his mates from a photo shoot, but still.

"Even if I was condescending, your prick of an ex deserved it." The vehemence with which the words came out of Alex's mouth shocked me.

"What did he ever do to you? He's fine…." I waffled, truly puzzled. "A bit of a party animal, but fine."

"That's exactly what it was. He's a bit wild. A bit fine." Alex ran a hand through his hair and, pushing off the bed, paced the length of the room. "You shouldn't have been with a guy like him. You weren't a good match."

"Okay." I blinked. "Desperately trying not to take offense on that."

Alex rolled his eyes.

"For fuck's sake, Alex, he was a model. Come on!"

On the path outside our tent, someone coughed. Ah, well, at least with the yelling, no one needed to worry about animals wandering through the campsite.

Alex's eyes darted toward the tent entrance, and he took a deep breath. "That's not what I meant, Nikki. It was the other way around. He wasn't good enough for you."

I scoffed. "Sure, that's really believable coming from you."

"I'm serious. You deserve a guy so much better than that." He was on the move again, arms gesturing. "No one's good enough for you."

"No one?" I asked, watching in fascination as he turned and paced back.

"No one, literally. Maybe if Michelangelo's David came to life and he was a volunteer doctor solving the maternal mortality crisis in Sierra Leone and he farted lilacs and his cum tasted like … like treacle and, of course, his cock would be huge…." He trailed off and turned to me, completely bewildered at my reaction.

I had giggled at "farts" because, well, I might be a little juvenile. But by the end of his speech, I'd bent over laughing.

His face was flushed, and he looked at me for a moment before slouching down onto the edge of the bed.

"What are you on about?" I asked between fits.

"Your perfect man."

"Doesn't sound like the perfect man to me. Sounds like he's got a stick up his arse." I wiped a tear away from my eye. For a day that had clearly ticked Alex off, I'd found most of it hilarious. "He farts lilacs?"

Alex's expression turned sheepish. "That's what every woman wants, right?"

He waited patiently while I got myself under control.

"I guess," he said, "that I was never keen on Ion, and perhaps I wasn't the nicest person to him."

My lips were still tipped up in a smile. "No, you weren't."

"Nor you, I suppose. I was a bit of a twat."

My smile fell, and I studied Alex. He was serious, now, honest. He meant it, but there was something there, too, that still burned.

Jealousy.

Alex was still jealous of Ion, even though we'd broken up months ago, even if he hadn't been right for me.

"What about you?" The question burst out of me.

He cocked his head at me. "What do you mean?"

Where was I going with this? Alex and I...well, we had tried once, at that dreadful party, but it was years ago, and we were different people now. On paper, when I stripped away his competitiveness and jealousy, I was left with an Alex I liked.

I didn't see that Alex all that often, but still.

I took a step closer to Alex. "What kind of a man would you be for me?"

His expression shifted. No longer bewildered and angry, the heat transformed into something else. Those eyes pulled me a step closer. My thigh touched his knee.

Alex swallowed and looked up at me. "I would be the best

kind of man for you." I watched his Adam's apple as it moved, the sharpness of it making me want to trail a finger over the taunt skin.

"You don't fart lilacs," I whispered.

He didn't even giggle. "How do you know?"

"Then you do an excellent job at hiding them. How about the cum thing?"

Alex's hand slid off his thigh and onto mine, bare below the hem of my skirt, his firm touch gripping the back of my knee.

"I hate to report that it doesn't taste like treacle."

I raised an eyebrow, and then I gave in, trailing a finger over his throat.

He swallowed hard.

I let that finger trail back up the side of his neck, spreading my hand out. My thumb slid up underneath his chin, and the skin was soft and smooth. Alex wasn't a hairy man, something I found attractive. Ion, being Romanian, had had to work hard to maintain his smooth skin.

My eyes traveled up to his lips, and my thumb followed. His mouth opened for me, and I traced slowly over his bottom lip.

Alex squeezed the back of my thighs hard. "Nikki…" His voice came out rusty and gritty.

I met his eyes, those dark eyes full of an intensity I'd never seen before. Alex and I were all about being fierce with each other, but here he was open, vulnerable.

Bending down, I pressed my mouth to his, closing my eyes. His grip tightened again, a sharp inhale draining out of both of us.

And then we were kissing; hot, wet, open kisses. This was nothing like that first kiss ages ago. This kiss gave that kiss a wedgie and shoved it in a locker. This was Kissing 401: How Alex Boyd Brought on the Rise and Fall of Nikki Kozlova.

Alex was a *good* kisser. *We* were good together. With just the right amount of tongue, our mouths synchronized perfectly.

His hands slid around to the inside of my thighs, tugging me gently. I let Alex pull me over him, sliding my knees up onto the mattress on either side of his hips. Alex ran his hands up my thigh, groaning when he found how far up my dress had risen with the spreading of my knees.

But we didn't stop. My hands were in Alex's hair, one of his hands pressed on my back, encouraging me to get closer to him, my full front to his, my breasts pressed hard against his chest, and the hem of my tight dress digging into my thighs. Impatiently I broke away, Alex's mouth following mine, his eyes dazed. I hiked my dress up to my waist and pressed closer, widening the stance.

Alex grunted his approval and pulled me to him again. And then we were down, down, down on the bed, thrusting and pressing and grinding…

And then the drums beat.

We broke apart, panting our own rhythm, staring at each other wide-eyed.

"Dinner," I said inelegantly.

"Right."

He made no effort to move, and our mouths were only millimeters away from each other.

I dropped down, unable to resist. This time our kisses were softer, our mouths closed.

In between, Alex remarked again, "Dinner."

I sighed. "Is that your way of telling me to get off?"

He grinned and thrust up against me, hard and ready and in just the perfect spot.

"You can take that either way you want."

I bent down and kissed him again. And again. And again until he flipped me over.

"Nikki," he said, nuzzling my nose with his. "We do need to eat. And we'll come right back here after dinner, yeah?"

"*You* have to eat."

Alex rolled away from me and sat on the edge of the bed. "Fairly certain you can't live off of my kisses. Plus, someone will be by any minute now to make sure we haven't been eaten by a leopard or run over by a hippopotamus."

"Fine."

We stayed quiet for a moment, him sitting on the edge of the bed, me sprawled out on the duvet, hair a mess.

"What are you doing?" he asked me.

"Recovering. What are you doing?"

"Waiting for my blood to spread back out."

"Good plan."

ELEVEN

It took us so long to recover that someone did try to come and find us. Alex assured Misola we were on our way, but because it was dark now, she waited at the tent entrance like a chaperone at a school dance. She may not have known what was going on, but I'm certain she would have noticed if we'd collapsed back into bed.

We sat at the long dining table, everyone else well into their beverage of choice. The fire was roaring, the lodge a bubble of warmth and chatter and merriment.

Alex and I sat next to each other, the last two seats available, saved just for us.

"We were waiting for you! Thought maybe you'd gotten distracted," said Mark, who sat across from me. He grinned slyly.

Olivia chimed in next to him. "I saw your dress, Nikki. It was lovely."

"Thank you. We were just…cleaning up," I said. Alex squeezed my thigh under the table. I had changed into a pair of leggings, but the feel of Alex's bare hand on my thigh flashed through my mind.

The meal came out—kudu steaks and peri-peri chicken—and we all tucked in.

"Did you enjoy a quiet day back here at the lodge?" Meino asked me.

"Yes," I said between bites of the perfectly cooked steaks.

"What did you do all day?"

Next to me, Alex grunted in response to something Mark said. He was methodically cutting into his chicken, chewing, swallowing, and on to the next bite.

I put another forkful of steak into my mouth, and though it was delicious, I couldn't help lamenting that it was something I really had to chew. Give me a meal replacement smoothie that I could chug down while on my way back to the tent. Then I could get back to kissing Alex.

Kissing Alex.

I replayed that line over and over again in my head. *Kissing Alex. Kissing Alex. I wanted to kiss Alex.*

The clatter of dishes and conversations around me quieted, and I realized I'd said that last bit out loud.

Alex laughed, as did the rest of the people at our table, and I hid my face behind my hands. Everyone very politely returned to their conversation, although I think I heard someone slap Alex's back.

Meino cleared his throat and repeated his question, his own cheeks pink, too, and there was still a half-chewed piece of steak in my mouth.

I chewed my too-big bit and fanned my face while I swallowed. "Took photos, enjoyed the pool, tried not to be a bother to the staff." I cast about for a topic that would keep Meino chatty so I could finish my meal and get the hell out of there, now running in mortification and haste to get Alex back to bed. "What did you see on the safari today?"

That worked a treat. Meino was off on a tangent, telling me about everything they'd spotted. Zebras, hyenas, even the kudu—not the one on my plate, thankfully.

I used my fork to scrape up the last bite of meat and set my napkin on the table next to my plate while I chewed. Alex still had a few bites left, and I reached over to grip his thigh.

Chew faster, don't choke.

Alex set his fork down, leaving the last few bites. I kicked my foot up, starting to swing over the bench seat to make our escape, only to run directly into Rowena's stomach. It was a good thing I hit her soft center and not the camera mere millimeters from my head.

"Oh, Nikki, I just have to show you the photos from today. I couldn't quite get the depth of field you were telling me about yesterday. Could you remind me of the settings?"

Behind her, Alex grimaced.

"Umm..." She looked up at me, blinking, her eyes so kind. I remembered the way she'd talked about wanting to preserve her memories.

I stifled a sigh. "Let me see."

Rowena clicked through her photos, and I checked the data and walked her through the aperture mode again.

Conrad cleared his throat. "Rowena, I think these kids want to get moving." He nodded his head to where Alex hovered.

I glanced back, and Alex's cheeks were flushed in the firelight.

"Oh, dear. Right, we can chat tomorrow, maybe during brunch? You'll be with us tomorrow, won't you, Nikki?"

"Yes, most definitely."

She nodded resolutely. "Good. We'll have a lesson then."

I turned, and Alex grabbed my hand, hurrying me along.

"Have fun, kids!" Conrad bellowed behind us. Alex's hand squeezed mine, and we raced out into the night.

For safety, we still had to have a guide walk us out to our tent, which felt like an awkward reverse walk of shame. Alex bumped shoulders with me as we tried not to mow down Misola.

Alex and I called goodnight to her and listened while she padded down the boardwalk back to the main lodge. A lone lamp cast shadows around the tent walls.

I glanced at Alex, his dark eyes pools of black in the dark lighting. He took a step toward me, his palm coming up to my cheek. He cupped my face, and I turned into his hand, nuzzling the thin skin at his wrist and feeling his pulse under my lips, the beat fast and strong.

Alex licked his lips before sliding his hand further, tangling his fingers in my hair and gripping the back of my neck, tugging me under him. When I gasped, he slid his lips over mine.

His grip tightened in my hair, the only sign he gave me of tension. His kiss was the opposite: slow embers, teasing and savoring. With one arm banded around my waist, Alex backed me up against the bed.

I broke away, sitting on the edge of the mattress, and Alex's hands came around my waist, pushing me up towards the pillows. He climbed beside me and gently brushed a stray hair away from my lips.

His finger trailed over my skin, around my ears, down the column of my neck, his eyes following the same course.

"You are so beautiful," he whispered, so earnest, so tender.

As he traced my collarbone, I slid my hand to his side, gripping his shirt, and lightly tugged.

Alex came forward, letting his lips brush mine gently before opening me again to his tongue. Hands lingered, small kisses, nips of teeth. It was all such a slow dance.

Time passed. Hours, days, years. Despite the tenderness, I ached. Alex was pressed against one side of me, our legs intertwined. My lips were swollen, my tongue tired, and I did not care one whit. I had never kissed anyone like this before. Like kissing was the only thing that mattered, an endgame to itself. Neither of us rushed—the kissing was just *too good.*

And part of me wondered if the rest of it was going to be exponentially better. That just didn't seem fair. How could one man be so good at kissing, and everything else too? Surely the universe wasn't that kind. Though I knew that Alex was an overachiever in many things, it wouldn't surprise me if he was just as good with his hands, his tongue, his cock.

"We should get ready for bed," Alex murmured in my ear. I hummed, but Alex wasn't committed to stopping. His lips dropped kisses along my neck, leaving me sighing.

"Do you really want to get up?"

"No, but if we don't, we're going to be zombies in the morning." He kissed his way back up. "Maybe we should sit out of the drive tomorrow."

I groaned as his lips teased mine again. They ached a little, but I definitely did not want him to stop. "I can't sit out the drive tomorrow. I already missed today."

"Mmm, yes, you did. You naughty girl."

I laughed as Alex tried to kiss me, making him laugh too. "Do you have a naughty girl fantasy?"

"I have a *you* fantasy."

"Yeah?" I tilted my head, looking up at him.

Alex propped himself up on his elbows, relieving me of most of his weight—except where it really mattered. I squirmed against his erection. He shifted back, and I whimpered.

The corner of his lips tilted up, but his eyes stayed serious. "Nikki, you're beautiful, kind, and funny. I've always had a thing for you." We stared at each other for a moment before Alex blinked. "Come on, let's actually get some sleep."

He pushed off the bed and helped me up too. We brushed our teeth, side by side, watching each other in the mirror and trying not to laugh. I spilt foam down onto my top.

As we tapped our toothbrushes and rinsed, Alex caught my eye again. "I really should shower."

"Me too. You go first."

I slipped out and sat on the bed, fidgeting as I listened to Alex undress and start up the shower. Without his body over mine, his lips on me, the cold seeped in, and by the time he was out, I was shivering under the covers.

He walked out in nothing but a towel, and I was momentarily distracted by the expanse of goose pimple-covered skin but shook it off. My shower was quick and hot, and I dressed, again, turned off the lights, and slipped under the covers.

And Alex found me, his lips landing on mine like they'd missed me as much as mine had missed his.

"So much for getting to bed," I said into the dark between kisses.

Alex's chuckle skimmed across my lips. "Sleeping is overrated."

TWELVE

OH, THAT FIVE A.M. WAKE-UP DRUMMING WAS THE WORST. AT least this time, I hadn't woken up to Alex jerking away from me. Instead, he'd had an arm around my waist, his body hard and pressed against me as we started to stretch and grumble.

We had stumbled around, getting our gear ready for the ride and drinking our hot tea. Once I'd had a few sips and moved around enough to wake up, I looked back at Alex, and he gave me a shy smile. It was like a dream. Had that all really happened?

And then he leaned over and kissed me again, and yes, yes it had.

Bundled up in the back of the Jeep, I fell asleep against Alex as we drove into the morning. He carefully nudged me awake when we had our first sighting.

After we snapped photos and Thomas moved us on, Alex leaned toward me, his breath against my ear making me shiver. "Do you think we need to hide this? From everyone else?"

I pushed my lips to the side, thinking. "I don't see any reason to. I mean, these people are only going to be in our lives for a few more days."

"Ah, well, I meant when we get back home."

"Oh. *Oh.* Oh my god, our mothers are going to be unbearable."

Alex chuckled next to me. "What, you mean they'll be proved right, and we'll never hear the end of it for the rest of our lives?"

"Exactly."

We bounced along quietly for a moment before I spoke what was on my mind. "I mean…what is this?"

Alex twisted in his seat to look at me fully. "I want to take you on a date when we get back home."

"A date?" I asked, eyebrows raised.

"A date." He nodded as the Jeep bounced. "To start." His eyes darted to me, and a slow smile tugged at his lips. I held his gaze, my own cheeks flushing.

And Alex reached across the seat and tangled his fingers with mine.

———

WE BUMPED ALONG THE ROAD ON OUR AFTERNOON DRIVE. IN THE backseat, I leaned my head on Alex's shoulder. Despite literally sitting all day, my stomach was starting to rumble, so I hoped we were getting close to our sunset cocktail location.

So far, we'd seen elephants, giraffes, jackals, hyenas, all sorts of birds, a dung beetle rolling his pile of poo (which was very, very entertaining), and an elusive leopard camped out in a tree, difficult to see despite the lack of foliage.

All in all, quite the day.

Alex kissed the crown of my head and rested his cheek against me. Sitting in the back with him all day had been lovely; lots of hand-holding, our shoulders and thighs pressed together in the cold of the morning, but once the air warmed up and we put the blankets away, it was only my thigh against his. At one point, I'd tucked my left foot under my right leg, letting my knee rest on Alex's lap, and he'd gotten to learn every single bit of my inner thigh—at least, the appropriate parts. When he got up to the hem of my shorts, I reliably shivered, and he strolled back down again so casually, gazing out the open car into the wilderness.

After a few passes, he let his pinky finger slip under my shorts, meandering along.

I shifted, lifting my head up to rest my chin on his shoulder.

"Just out of curiosity, do you have any condoms?"

The pinky went still. Alex turned to look at me as best he could. "No, I don't. Do we need some?"

"Well." I waggled my head. "Monkeys ate my birth control."

His lips flickered, suppressing a smile. "One only requires birth control if one is having sex."

"Oh, is that how it works?" I deadpanned. "Good god, I've been using condoms wrong this whole time."

Ah, then he did laugh, that big wide smile that was new and familiar at the same time. "Okay, so we don't have condoms. Should we try to find some?"

I bit my lip and dipped my chin. "I think we could do other things."

Alex's lashes fluttered, and he squeezed my thigh. "I like other things. I like other things a lot."

"What kind of other things do you like?" I whispered.

"I like kissing you." His voice had dropped low, and his tongue dipped out to wet his lips. "I like the noises you make and how I can feel the heat of you through our clothes. I dream about the way you're going to sound when I'm inside of you. With my fingers or my tongue or my cock."

My thigh muscles tensed under his fingers, and a sigh passed my lips. "I can't wait to make noises for you."

He kneaded the muscles of my thigh. "Do you like dirty talk, Nikki?"

I nodded, entranced. The other passengers, the bumps of the dirt road underneath us, the soft murmuring of Thomas up front—they all faded away.

Alex's other hand came up and tilted my chin toward his. His long fingers swept up my cheek, and he pressed his lips to mine, so lightly. I kissed him back, and we both kept our mouths open, soft and gentle. I ran my hand up his side, feeling the way his muscles shifted underneath my hand, his ribs expanding with every breath as his body stretched toward me. Still, our lips were light and gentle until I felt Alex's tongue slip out and trace my bottom lip…

With a soft bump, the car came to a halt.

"Okay, everyone. Here's our spot for sunset," Thomas called out. "Stretch your legs, and we'll have cocktails ready in no time."

Alex and I pulled away, grinning at each other. He gave me one more squeeze before turning and opening the door. I followed him out, accepting his hand as I stepped down.

I took a look around. The other two Jeeps were parked nearby, all of the guests together for sunset this time. We were on a small hill overlooking a watering hole. A few barren trunks stretched out of the water, and one of them even had a nest on the highest V of the branches. The water was still, no animals in sight, and we had the perfect view for sunset.

Pulling out my gear from the Jeep, I set up my tripod. With the calm, still waters and the dying light, I might be able to get a really nice long exposure photo.

Alex sidled up to me a few minutes later with a gin and tonic as I tested out my exposures. He stood behind me, watching me work, his body lightly pressed against my back, especially against my hips.

When I straightened up, he rested his chin on my shoulder, his hands on either side of me, holding our drinks. I took the one in his right hand and used my remote clicker to snap some photos. The bar was on the left side of the frame with the chairs and people around it, and the lake, farther out in the distance, took up the other half of the shot.

The camera took a few seconds, and when it popped up on the back screen, the people were blurry with movement, but the pond eerily still.

"Whoa," Alex whispered in my ear. "How do you do that?"

I explained the setting I used, keeping the shutter open as long as possible without letting the photo overexpose. I was a bit nervous telling him this, but my excitement took over for me.

"You are very good at that," he said, kissing my hair.

"Thank you." I blushed, taking a sip of my cocktail.

"I'm going to, uh, socialize. Have fun."

I released the breath I was holding. Alex didn't seem to be too interested in the details. Maybe I'd found a skill he had no interest in gaining for himself?

Or maybe his days of crashing my hobbies were over. Perhaps, with us forming a real relationship, we could move on from our rivalry.

I fiddled with my camera more, adjusting settings as the sky got darker. Thomas had lit a few lanterns around, and the contrasting light added more drama to the photos.

It was almost time to get going; daylight was fading, and we were due back to the lodge before true dark. Rex was packing up the seats, and I was about to put my camera away when I heard a gasp from the other guests.

I looked up and followed the direction of Ernst's finger pointing out toward the lake. In the very last glow of daylight, an elephant walked out of the brush. We'd seen plenty of the gentle giants on our drives over the previous days, but we still all hummed and chattered appreciatively as we watched the animal come to the edge of the water and sway its trunk back and forth, investigating.

But then I noticed a bit of movement past the hindquarters, and out came a baby elephant, trotting to catch up and nearly stumbling into the water. We all gasped—the little one was truly the cutest animal I'd ever seen in real life. The mother flapped her ears as the baby splashed around.

I quickly changed a few settings and took a shot, but I knew the light was fading too much. Maybe I'd be able to work up something in processing, but this moment would have to be enjoyed out from behind the camera, being in the moment, something I couldn't share with anyone else. A moment just for our group.

And that made it all the more special.

THIRTEEN

WE ALL WANTED TO LINGER AND WATCH THE TWO ELEPHANTS, but Thomas had to hustle us along so we'd be out of the park when it closed and back at the lodge for dinner. Climbing back into the Jeep, I tucked my gear away, and Alex accepted a blanket to throw over our laps. I shivered. The temperature had dropped quickly while we'd stood and watched the elephants.

Thomas started the car up, and Alex lifted an arm so I could snuggle in next to him.

"Did you get any shots of the elephants?" he asked.

I stifled a yawn. "Probably not. Too dark."

"Yeah," he agreed. "I don't think we've been out this late. That must be a hard part of the job for Thomas and Rex, having to rope the guests back in when it's time to go, no matter what's out there."

"True. It's a balance of the experience versus responsibility."

"It is rather dark back here," Alex noted, shifting around. He turned his head slightly to whisper in my ear. "And we've got this nice blanket covering us up."

Fingers slipped over my knee, trailing a slow path up my inner thigh. I hummed in approval and shifted my knees further apart.

Alex kissed my temple and kept his lips there. Warm puffs of air disturbed the wisps of hair around my temple. Fingers slowly trailed up and up and up…

He traced the band of my underwear, just barely grazing my lips. Surely, he could feel the heat and dampness already, and I squirmed in anticipation. In response, he brought the rest of his fingers around my upper thigh.

"I like the way your skin feels." He rotated his hand, running all his fingers along the edge now. Then, so slowly, a finger slid from the side, over my panties, and to my center. Alex inhaled sharply, letting his finger press against me. "I like the way that feels even better."

He began to draw small circles, feeling his way around to find just the right spot. When I gasped in response, I felt him smile against my temple.

"Right there," he said, sounding smug.

My hand trailed across to his lap, where I fumbled for a minute, and he shifted to give me some room. I brushed his erection with the back of my hand and then attempted to wrap my fingers around him. I giggled when the leggings he wore under the shorts provided little give, and my hand slipped off.

He laughed, too, but then pulled me close. Quietly, we kissed, his finger still running in slow circles in just the right spot. I had to pull back, needing more air, but he kept me pressed against him. I could barely make out his face in the dark anymore.

But both our bodies surged forward when the Jeep came to a halt. I would have been face-first on the Jeep floor if it hadn't been for Alex holding me in place.

"Okay, everyone," Thomas said. "We're a bit late, so

you've only got fifteen minutes to freshen up. See you back at the bar."

Alex and I slipped our hands out, but when I went to stand up, Alex stopped me. Keeping eye contact, he slipped his finger—*the* finger—in his mouth and moaned around it.

"Back to the tent. Now." I shoved him out the Jeep door, and he caught himself, laughing. He offered his hand to help me down, and once my feet were on the ground, we wound our fingers together and briskly walked along the boardwalk.

"Nikki!"

My stomach plummeted in disappointment as we came to a halt.

Sam caught up to us. "Sorry, you are later than I expected, so I didn't catch you right out of the Jeep. Could you come with me very quickly and bring your camera?"

"Uh, well…" I glanced at Alex.

"That's okay. I'll see you back at the tent." His hand squeezed mine three times, and then he let go.

Sam led me to the kitchen, where the staff had set up a few more plates for me to photograph. I made quick work of it, hoping to be back at the tent for…a quickie? A shower? Honestly, I was willing to show up to dinner absolutely filthy.

Alex Boyd was a tease.

Unfortunately, the drums banged for dinner, and I was still shooting the last plate. When I finished, I crashed out of the kitchen, nearly running into Alex.

"Hey, is everything okay?" His hair was still damp from a shower, and he'd changed while I was occupied.

"Yes," I said, gesturing over my shoulder. "Sam wanted me to take some pictures for her. I'm going to head back to the tent, quickly."

Alex held out a hand. "I can take your bags back if you want to stay here. I'm afraid you probably don't have time to shower."

"You could take my bags back," I said, stepping in close to Alex and dropping my voice. "But you can't change my panties for me."

A noise that sounded an awful lot like "ughnnnaaa" came out of Alex's mouth as he flopped his forehead onto my shoulder. "I didn't need to know that. The last thing I want to do is to be chatting with Ernst or Mark over a cocktail and a hard-on."

I shoved him off me playfully. "Dinner won't last forever. I'll be back."

As Alex shuffled over to the bar, a little stiff-legged, I walked out to the tent and dropped off my gear and made the aforementioned panty swapping. I was the last one to arrive back at the dining hall, and since Alex already had a drink for me, I took my seat.

Dinner was delicious, and I debated about suggesting we leave right away, but then dessert came out, and, well, if I had to choose between orgasms, dessert, or sleep, I'd be a well-fed, sleep-deprived zombie tomorrow.

The dessert was malva pudding, a South African classic that literally had me scraping the plate clean. I debated licking it, too, but while I knew Alex well, I didn't know what his turn-offs might be. Plate-licking was too risky of a line to cross.

Alex made that noise again. "Ughnnnaaa."

"So that's a general blissed-out noise and not a sign of your sexual desires. Good to know."

He contemplated his empty plate and the spoon in his hand, looking rather forlorn. "I'm not saying it was as good as sex. But…"

"I think we should head back to the tent before you finish that statement." I stood up, tugging Alex along with me.

We said our goodnights and rolled ourselves—they were big portions of dessert—back to the tent.

I switched on the lights, stripping off my outer layers, and Alex immediately tried to tug me toward the bed. "Oh, don't," I said, sounding prissy, even to my own ears. "I'm still all dirty from the drive."

"Someone was too busy with their camera to shower, unlike myself, who is squeaky clean."

"Well then, I guess you won't be showering with me."

Alex grinned. "I can guess exactly what would happen in that scenario. We'd be in the shower together, get distracted, the well water would run out, and everyone would hate us because there'd be no water for the rest of our stay."

I laughed and smacked his arm. "Right then, off I go. You can keep the bed warm."

"You seem to be mistaken. I'm not showering with you, but I *am* watching."

"Excuse me?" I said, mock-affronted.

"If I'm invited to shower with you, I'm invited to watch. Or, at the very least, perform my ablutions in the same room as you showering. Anything to get us moving faster."

He hauled me off the bed and frog-marched me into the washroom. Alex stood at the sink with his toiletry bag, digging through for floss and toothpaste. I met his eyes in the mirror and raised an eyebrow.

He raised one back, and I swept my shirt off over my head. We held eyes while I moved to my shorts, unbuttoning them and letting them drop to the floor. I broke eye contact to pull my sports bra off over my head, and Alex's hands slowed while twining his floss around a finger. His gaze held mine again.

I dug my thumbs under the waistband of my underwear, and a muscle twitched in his cheek. His hands had completely stopped moving. In this game of chicken, I was winning.

I dropped my underwear. Alex blinked. And then

dropped his gaze to run, very thoroughly, up and down my body.

Wait. Did I win? Or did he?

I ducked the question by climbing into the shower stall. I washed quickly, and when I stepped out, Alex waited with a towel.

He was naked, the towel outstretched to wrap around me, conveniently hiding his goods.

He gently ran the towel over my face, pushing my hair back. The expression had shifted from horny to tender, and he toweled me off, rubbing my arms and back.

He twisted the towel around to my back and pulled it closed between us.

This time I broke, looking him up and down. Alex was all long and lean, the body of a man who worked out fastidiously for the health benefits and probably ignored a few too many meals while he worked.

He was hard, too, his cock bobbing between us. I let him hold the towel while I wrapped a hand around him. Alex tugged the towel, pulling me closer and reaching down to kiss me.

The kiss was languid until I squeezed my fist, and Alex threw the towel off behind me and scooped me up, carrying me to bed.

I bounced lightly on the bed. "We don't have condoms."

Alex pressed a kiss to my lips first before answering in deadpan, "Oh no. We'll have to do other things."

He reared back, tugging the duvet and linens out from under me. I raised my hips to help, and once we were both clear, Alex threw the covers back over us.

There was no preamble, no lazy meandering; Alex's mouth was between my legs in an instant. I gasped, the shock of it warm and wet.

Alex liked to take things slow in all aspects of his life, and regardless of how fast his mouth had gotten there, he did not rush. He taunted and teased and slipped a finger in and then two until I was panting and shifting. Only then did he back off, kissing the smooth inside of my thighs and working his way up. His fingers stayed where they were, and I clenched around them.

My nipples were taut under the sheets, and Alex played with them, using teeth and tongue while pumping his hand.

"Alex," I croaked out, "I can't come without clit stimulation.

"Well," he drawled, "right now, I'm not trying to make you come."

I groaned and closed my eyes, letting my head fall back. Alex kept up the stroking, kept teasing my nipples, building me up. And then suddenly, he was gone.

I opened my eyes to find him hovering over me, his arms straight and planted on either side of my head. His lips were curved in a wide, naughty smile. "God, you are beautiful."

My hands grasped both sides of his body, feeling the ribs expand and collapse underneath. "You say such sweet things when you're torturing me."

He laughed, dropping down to his elbows. "Is it really that bad?"

"So bad it's good."

"Can I keep going?"

I looked at the clock beside me. "We have five hours until we get woken up by the drums and our days are packed. We really do need to manage our sleep for the rest of the trip."

"And then we go back to the real world."

We both waited, silent for a few moments.

"Do it again," I said breathlessly.

And he did, disappearing under the covers, sliding fingers inside me and applying his mouth until I bowed off the bed, just on the edge.

Then he disappeared, a breeze stirring around my heated

body while he came back up. When he plopped down on the pillow next to me, we were both panting.

"Do I get to do this to you next?"

"Teasing me? Unlikely." He grinned. "But you can try."

He kissed me, told me how beautiful I was, how good I tasted, more sweetness until he decided it was time. Back down he went, and this time his attention was more focused. His tongue swirled, his fingers slipping in and pressing me exactly where I needed it.

I writhed against his face, the sheets slipping down and the cool air chasing goosebumps across my skin. The pressure buildup was intense, aching, and when he started to pull away, I clamped my thighs down. His breath ghosted my skin as he laughed between my legs.

"Shhh. Okay, okay," he chanted.

When I relaxed, he dove back in and kept pushing me until my abdomen curled in and my body clenched around him, coming while great big waves of tension released through me.

Gently, he pulled his fingers out, then kissed his way up until we were eye to eye.

"You just have to be the best at everything, don't you?"

"At making you come, absolutely."

He lay next to me while I caught my breath, and he let my hand wander down to his cock to grip it. He was hard and heavy, a bead of pre-cum dripping onto my fingers. The heat was intense, and in a bout of energy, I pushed him down, rising over him and slipping him into my mouth, just like he'd done to me, sinking right into the feel and taste of him.

And with a muffled cry, he came. I swallowed him down, gently sucking until he twitched and pulled me up.

"Jesus fucking Christ, that was embarrassing."

"Well," I said, cleaning my mouth off with my fingers, "can confirm, you don't taste like treacle."

He laughed. "You didn't believe me? Too bad for you."

I slipped off the bed and immediately shivered in the cold. Alex followed, and we brushed our teeth side by side at the sink, eyes all over each other.

Back in bed, Alex let me settle in on my side and then curled around me. "That was perfect."

FOURTEEN

THE NEXT FEW DAYS PASSED BY BEAUTIFULLY. THE DRIVES WERE entertaining and exhausted us every day. Every opportunity we had in the tent or in the back of the Jeep, we'd make out, saving the best for the end of the day, providing our own heat under the blankets.

I had an obscene number of photographs from the drives, but I had no idea if they were good enough yet; I hadn't pulled out my laptop to check.

Finally, it was our last day in Kruger. We had different flights booked back to London, and Alex offered to switch his itinerary to be with me.

"It's fine, don't go through the trouble," I said as we rode on our way to the airport.

"Sick of me already?"

I pressed a kiss to his smooth cheek. "Not nearly. Your flight lands a few hours before mine, though, so should I come over to your place when I land?"

"Well, actually, er…." He looked at his watch and did some mathematical gymnastics. "Time zones, red-eye…I get in on Sunday?"

"Right. Today's Saturday, and you've got a red-eye."

"I've got dinner with my parents that night. We always have Sunday night dinner."

"Of course, you do. And then you'll need to go to bed early and get back to the workforce on Monday."

Alex winced. "Yes, the emails are piling up, I'm sure. You could join us for dinner?"

I thought for a moment. "No, I've just had you for a week. I'll let your parents enjoy some quality time with you."

Natasha Boyd was a superb mother, as I'd seen growing up. I'd always been a little jealous of Alex with his mother, and they'd continued their close relationship as we became adults. I could never work for my mother or father, but it seemed to work out pretty well for Alex and Natasha.

It was surely nepotism to start, but Alex did a damn fine job at her company, working in the User Experience department. And he had been promoted—several times.

Alex had a space in the world, and he knew where he belonged: at Boyd Technologies, with his parents, with his schoolmates.

What was I going back to? Unlike Alex, I hadn't kept up with our schoolmates, and now Ion's friends were no longer mine. My mother and I had a regular weekly phone call, but she was busy being a socialite. And Father...well, I had never really known what Father did, and I didn't really want to learn now. It was probably best if I didn't know.

Alex grinned at me. "You just don't want to tell our mothers we're together now."

I threw my hands up. "They're going to be horrid! All smug and thinking they were right all along."

He laughed. "You know I'm going to tell Mum tonight, right?"

"Yes, and she'll call my mother and celebrate."

Alex laced his fingers through mine. "I actually have something for you, to celebrate too."

"Oh? You have my attention."

Alex reached into the backpack at his feet and pulled out a bracelet. It was one I recognized from our village tour, made of carved bone and porcupine quills the locals had strung together.

"Alex." My heart melted a little bit. "We hadn't even kissed yet. You bought this for me?"

He shrugged, a blush creeping up his ears. "I wanted you to have something—aside from photographs—to remember the trip by."

I leaned over and kissed his cheek, slipping the bracelet on my wrist. "Thank you."

We arrived at the airport and gave a flurry of hugs and handshakes to Thomas. Alex and I had discussed the tips in advance, and Alex handed the envelope to him as we said goodbyes.

After a brief check-in, we were seated at the gate. Alex nudged me.

"There's Wi-Fi here," he said, gesturing with his phone.

I glanced down at his phone. "Back to reality?"

Alex looked down too. He took a deep breath. "Yes. Back to the real world, with a job and a work schedule and not enough free time."

I pulled out my phone, queueing up the connection. I nodded, decisive. "Let's do it."

"Wait, wait." He wrapped an arm around me pulling me close to him and ducking to meet my lips. The armrest of my seat dug into my ribs, but when Alex kissed me, I could have been on fire and wouldn't have given a whit.

After what was probably indecently long for a public kiss in an airport, we broke apart.

"One last kiss before we go back to the real world."

Right, the real world where Alex is a Very Busy Person.

He turned his attention back to his phone, and I almost shouted out, "No! Wait! Stop! Let's just run off into the African savanna and never return again."

But of course, I didn't. Real life called.

And the pings started to come in on Alex's phone. He sighed and ran his hand through his hair, beginning to scroll through the messages.

I turned back to my phone and tapped Connect. It vibrated, messages coming in too. Not nearly the backlog Alex had, but enough.

We sat in silence, scanning messages, typing out responses, and carried on like that through the flight and while I walked with Alex to his gate in Joburg. Alex's brows furrowed more with every step we took toward home.

"Take a seat," he said, gesturing to the waiting area. "I have to make a call."

I took his bag and settled in. He typed a few moments on his phone and then turned and walked away, holding the phone to his ear. "Hi, Mum."

Rather than turning back to my phone, I watched Alex. He paced near the washrooms, talking animatedly to Natasha, tucking his hand into his pockets while he listened and then pulling it out to gesture as he talked. I bit my lip, trying not to laugh. He looked up and caught my eye, giving me a lopsided smile that made my heart melt a little. An uncomfortable feeling I still wasn't used to having around him.

"So, I've got a bit of a problem," Alex interrupted me as I scrolled through my Instagram notifications. He took a seat next to me, tucking his phone back in his pocket.

I set my phone on my lap. "What's happened?"

"There was a bug discovered in some of the mobile application coding, and it's...well, it's screwed up a big project of ours for the software update coming out in four months. They've been working on a resolution, with the team staying late a lot. Mum's even been involved since I've been gone, but she's got a conference on women in technology later this week, so she really needs me there." He let out a big sigh, leaning back against the chair.

"You'll be busy, basically," I said.

"I will be busy. But we'll figure it out. I'll be able to take some time off next weekend, I hope," Alex said, harried.

"Hey," I said, placing my palm on his forearm. "I've got stuff to do too. I'm pretty self-sufficient, you'll find."

Alex looked doubtful. "It's not just this week, unfortunately. I'm busy a lot."

I rolled my eyes, picking up my phone. "Alex, I've known you for years, and in this case, you're the spitting image of your mother. I have plenty to do, but my schedule is more flexible. You just let me know when you're free, and I'll adjust."

He blinked at me. "What do you do all day? You clearly have me sorted out, but I must admit your life right now is a bit of a mystery to me."

"Oh, you know." I waved it off, feeling guilty for the first time. "Photo editing and Instagram." It wasn't a lie, but it was a half-truth.

His seating section was called over the intercom, and we stood up.

"Okay, so…" Alex started.

"I'll text you when I get home, and we'll figure out our schedule when you've got a better grasp on the office situation."

Alex's hands came up to cup my face. "You're pretty brilliant, you know?"

"We just spent a week together. We might benefit from some time apart anyway."

A frown marred Alex's face. "As long as we do see each other. Soon."

"Entirely up to you."

"Okay." Alex looked less confident now, but a queue was gathering, and he needed to board the plane.

"Kiss me," I demanded, and that seemed to relax him a

little bit. He stepped into me and slid his palms up my back, holding me close and easing his mouth over mine.

"See you soon," he whispered before breaking off and standing in the queue. I waved goodbye, gathered my own things, and departed for my gate. This would be fine. There was no way I would miss Alex, who'd only a week ago been a thorn in my side. Not when I had my own job to do.

FIFTEEN

Okay, I missed Alex. Not enough to be miserable, but still.

I had texted him when I had arrived home. He'd messaged back as I was unpacking, letting me know he'd woken up from a nap and was running late for dinner at his parents'. As tired as I was feeling, with a busy day's worth of travel behind me, I couldn't blame him.

Later, as I prepared for bed, I sent off another text. Alex responded.

ALEX

Still at my parents. Mum and I have moved to her home office.

The next two days went like that. We texted back and forth a bit, *I miss yous* and *goodnights*.

Finally, we made plans to have dinner together Wednesday night. I wasn't sitting around, pining for Alex—much. I kept myself busy, editing my photos, scheduling my social media, and talking with Siviwe, making sure that I was meeting expectations for our deliverables and giving her feedback on my trip. Then I was looking ahead to my next trip and sending out pitches for new ones.

I picked up my phone and took a few deep breaths, navigating to the contact information for one of the travel magazine editors I'd worked for in the past, summoning up the courage to make the call. What is it with my generation and the absolute hatred of talking on the phone?

I squared my shoulders and pressed the call button.

It rang a few times before an American voice answered. "This is Tessa."

"Tessa, hello, this is Nikki Kozlova. I wrote that article you published in your magazine on Chichen Itza?"

Her voice brightened. "Hey, yes, I remember you. Good to hear from you. It's been a few months since that issue came out, hasn't it?"

Seeing my photos and story in a major travel magazine had been surreal. I had been too nervous to pitch again, sure that, given time, someone was going to complain about a factual inaccuracy or write to the magazine about how terrible the article was. Imposter syndrome at its finest.

I took a deep breath. "It has been a while, but I wanted to talk to you about the trip I just took."

Tessa listened while I described my trip and outlined three possible stories she might be interested in. Since the stay was comped, I avoided talking about the lodge in general, but I had taken all of my experiences on the trip and researched several topics that I felt I could write feature articles on.

"It's been a while since you've featured a sub-Saharan region in the magazine, and that the lodge is owned by the tribe is important."

"It definitely is," Tessa agreed. "Why don't you work on the conservation article and put me in touch with your contact at the lodge? Send me some pictures to share with our team, and we will discuss it, but I think it's a great idea and your photos were a hit in the last article."

My body relaxed, and Tessa and I discussed some details

and logistics. "Hey," she said as the conversation was winding up. "You live in London, right?"

"I do. You're in the States?"

"I am now, but I'm moving to Europe for a year. I'll be mostly in Croatia, with a digital nomad visa, but I'll be traveling around too. I know Croatia is far from you, of course, but maybe we can meet if I come to London."

An opportunity to meet with someone as influential as Tessa?

"Yes," I breathed, trying to keep excitement out of my voice. "Absolutely. But...surely you know people in London?"

Tessa laughed. "I do, but you can never have too many good contacts. And maybe we can discuss your next article in person."

I might have swooned a tiny bit. "Lovely." My phone buzzed against my face.

"I'll let you know when that happens. I look forward to seeing your pictures, and we'll talk soon!"

We hung up, and I shook my head, dazed that Tessa not only remembered me but was looking forward to working with me again.

Then I remembered the text on my phone, and with a sinking heart, I opened up the message. It was from Alex.

ALEX

Nikki...we're still working. No end in sight. I have to cancel tonight.

I sighed. At least he was letting me know. I tapped my fingernail on the edge of my phone. I wanted to tell Alex about the call with Tessa, but I would have to explain so much. What have I gotten myself into?

Instead, I typed out a message back.

NIKKI

What if I brought lunch tomorrow?

When the phone rang, I assumed it would be Alex ringing to discuss lunch. Instead, it was my mother.

"Annika Elizaveta Kozlova," my mother began and gave me a tongue-lashing of Russian proportions, "how could you not tell me you and Alex are dating?"

When she calmed down enough, I filled her in on the mother-appropriate aspects of my new relationship, and she huffed at me. "I had to hear from Natasha!"

"I know, Mum. I'm sorry."

By the time I soothed Mum's ruffled feathers, I was yawning in exhaustion.

I brushed my teeth, and Alex finally responded with a gif of a kid jumping up and down in excitement.

NIKKI

Dork.

ALEX

Yes. Miss you.

———

Boyd Technologies took up the entire building, which was no surprise. This was their headquarters, and with billions in sales every year, they could afford a whole building, even in a prime location such as Camden and Islington.

The security desk buzzed me up, and rather than taking me right to Alex, Paige, the assistant who'd greeted me at the elevator, led me into a huge office with glass windows, a wide, mahogany desk, and a stunning view.

A leather couch sat against the interior wall, which was made of opaque glass that blocked the view and most of the light. I sat on the couch, resting the takeaway on the table in front of it, and waited.

I had been early but prepared. I had work to do, and I made a note to myself to ask Alex if I could use his desk to work the next time I came in to wait for him. I spent some time responding to emails and catching up on social media.

"Hey." Alex's voice hit me from the doorway.

I stood up, smoothing my sundress down as he took two long strides and wrapped his arms around me. The hug was a good one, long and the kind that lets you breathe someone in and sink into the way they smell. Alex pulled back, only to kiss me. Any hesitation I felt melted away; Alex and I just had to get into a groove together, figure out how to make two very busy people have a working relationship.

"Thank you so much for bringing lunch. What a treat," he said as we sat in the chairs in front of his desk. I opened up the containers of Thai food, and we tucked in. Alex explained some of the finer details of the project he was working on, and I told him about planning my upcoming trip to Sri Lanka.

"It's a yoga retreat in the highlands. Apparently, there's a chilly climate in the center of the island, and that's where tea was grown back in the day."

"So, you'll be drinking tea and doing yoga?"

"And sightseeing." For the first time, I felt a twinge of guilt. This was a lie by omission; I was leaving out that the retreat was arranging the trip for me.

"What kind of sightseeing?"

"There's a popular train ride, some historic sights. Safaris are popular there, too, but I won't be going on one."

Alex swallowed his bite of pad Thai. "I better find some time in my schedule to see you before you go, I should think."

"That would be nice, but don't feel too bad about this past week. I've been busy too." One of my pitches had responded positively, and I had nearly sealed the deal on a local event here in London. And I had organized my social media schedule for the next month. Plenty to be done.

"What have you been doing?" he asked.

That guilt hit me again. Alex was my boyfriend now, and he'd backed off a lot. Maybe we were both mature enough, or maybe being together for a whole week had soothed some need of Alex's to compete with me. "Actually, I've been working on—"

Alex's phone chirped. "Ah, shite. I've got my next meeting to go to." He grimaced at me. "Sorry." He stood up while shoveling another bite of noodles in. "Are you free on Friday? I can take the night off, but I will have to come into work on Saturday."

"Friday is good." At least with a freelance gig, I could work around Alex's schedule.

Alex held out a hand to me, and I set my food on the desk before he pulled me up. "It's a date, yes?" His arms slid around my waist and pulled me close to him.

"A date," I confirmed.

Alex flashed me a smile before slanting his mouth to mine. I opened to him and pressed close when the heat started to build.

He pulled back slightly. "I did go shopping, briefly, since I had to run into the Tesco anyway."

"Shopping?"

"Yes. I bought some condoms." His hands slid down to my hips, pressing me more firmly against his erection.

I ran my fingers up Alex's hair, and he groaned into the kiss.

"Alex!" Paige called out. "Your two p.m.!"

He sighed, pushing me away and adjusting himself. "Be right there." He tilted my chin up for a quick kiss. "Talk soon?"

"Soon."

SIXTEEN

FINALLY, FINALLY! WE WERE HAVING A DATE NIGHT. MY TRIP TO
Sri Lanka was an opportunity for Alex to work his adorable
arse off, and he was using that to justify taking a night off
work. We had reservations at one of my favorite restaurants, a
French bistro out in my borough, and Alex was on his way to
pick me up. The place wasn't that fancy, but I was too excited
and overdressed in a sleek black dress and ringlets in my hair.

I'd just finished putting on some lip shade when Alex
knocked, fifteen minutes early. I flung open the door, gratified
to see that Alex had dressed up too.

He looked me up and down, a slow smile spreading on
his lips. He sighed as he stepped inside, and I closed the door
behind him. He had a small black bag over one shoulder,
which he swung down to the floor. "Nikki, you look
fantastic."

Alex stepped into me, sliding his hands around my waist
and pulling me against him. His lips hovered over mine.

"Wait, I just put on lip…" I started. Alex paused. "You
know what? Never mind, I don't care."

I pulled his head down to me, and we met in a hungry
kiss. I leaned into him, and with a thump, Alex's back hit the

door. We took a deep inhale of each other, our bodies fully pressed together, and Alex's hands started to wander. One tangled in my hair, the other found the hem of my dress and swept underneath it. He groaned when he found my bare ass cheek and traced up to the band of thong at my hip.

My stomach fluttered, and I tipped my hips against his erection. Alex reached further down, palming his hand just below my knee and lifting up, spreading me open and hooking my leg on his waist.

I broke the kiss and moaned while Alex trailed kisses down the column of my neck.

"Don't we have a reservation to get to?" I gasped. He was doing something with his fingers now, sliding around from behind and running it up and down the entire thong.

"Yes, but I also bought condoms. And you look too fucking good in this dress. I think you should take it off."

I pushed him away as his fingers tried to climb up my back and find the zipper. "Call the restaurant and cancel, and I'll take this off."

Alex leaned back against the door and closed his eyes, tipping his head back and taking deep breaths.

"You can call them, even with an erection."

His lips screwed up. "No, I can't."

"They won't know, you know."

He looked at me, appalled. "I'll know!"

I pressed up against him, and he chuffed out a laugh before pushing me away. "You said you were going to take that off."

Pointedly, I looked down at his tented trousers. "That's not going to help your situation."

Alex closed his eyes again, and I leaned on my couch, waiting. After a minute or two, with noticeable tented trouser reduction, Alex pulled his phone out of his pocket and dialed.

"Yes, hello, I have a reservation in"—he checked his watch — "fifteen minutes and I'm not going to make it."

I raised my right hand to the opposite side of my body and raised my left arm to expose the zipper. Alex's eyes zoned in on my fingers, and I gripped the zipper and tugged downward.

His eyes widened the further down I got.

"Yes. Boyd."

Reaching the bottom, I let both hands fall to my hem and crossed my arms.

"Yes, for two people." His eyes narrowed.

I raised the hem of my dress, wiggling my hips as I brought the material up and over my head, letting my hair fall in a mess around my face. I shook my hair out and dropped the dress beside me. I stood in front of Alex, naked save for that thong he'd felt under my dress.

The phone fell away from Alex's ear, and I heard the tinny voice talking to him. He blinked, taking me in from my messy hair to my toes.

"No-sorry-I-can't-reschedule-must-go-now-bye." Clicking off, Alex tossed the phone on the couch behind me. "You," he said, tracing a palm over my hip, "look like you need a very good fucking."

And with that, he bent down and threw me over his shoulder. "Which way's your room?"

I squealed. "Alex! Put me down."

"Nope, can't. I'm choosing a door."

Alex stomped through the house in search of my bedroom, and as he made for one of the doors, I giggled. "Not that one."

He tilted his head to lightly gnaw on my ass cheek. "Cheeky. This one?"

I didn't answer and instead slid my hand down the back of his trousers.

Next thing I knew, I was being tossed onto my bed. The sheets were already a mess—I never managed to be one of those people who made their own bed every day, but I suspected Alex was—and I bounced gently before Alex was on me.

We kissed, deep and hot, before Alex started to trail his way down my body.

"No, no, absolutely not. Give me the condoms. Forget the foreplay."

Alex lifted his head up from where he'd been kissing my belly. "You sure?"

"Take my thong off. Feel how wet I am." I tipped my chin up.

Alex sat back on his knees—still fully dressed, mind you—and peeled the thong off before sliding a finger down my center.

He groaned and brought his finger to his mouth, sucking the whole digit clean. He bent down anyway, kissing my pussy. "I'll be back for you later," he whispered to it.

Standing, he peeled off his clothes with efficiency and started to climb back up on the bed. "Ack, wait, the condoms."

I got to watch Alex's lean ass disappear back into my hallway and return moments later with a whole strip of condoms.

I pointed at him. "On. Now."

"Are you sure? I feel morally obligated to make you come first."

"Well, I know you didn't make me orgasm at all while we were in Kruger," I deadpanned.

Alex huffed a laugh before tearing open the condom and rolling it on. He climbed up the bed between my legs and settled his weight on my hips, his cock long and hard against my core.

"My god," I said, exasperated. "You are such a tease, Alex." I pinched his side, and he squirmed against me, laughing. I pinched again, and whilst trying to fend me off, he grabbed my leg and hiked it up around his waist, plunging in with one stroke.

We both sucked in air, our laughter disappearing. Alex brought both hands up to my face, and I curled my legs around his, keeping us locked together. Feather-light, he dusted a kiss across my lips.

"You feel so good," he whispered, starting small rocking motions.

I pressed my lips against his, and his hands swept up into my hair as he deepened the kiss. We rocked together, kissing when we could, breathing when we had to.

I traced the bumps of his spine with my fingertips, feeling the muscles flex around me. Alex's skin became slick, his kisses less frequent.

"Nikki," he breathed. "I'm not going to last." He pressed his forehead against mine. "Are you close?"

"No, but that's okay."

He closed his eyes, nodding slightly. "I'll take care of you, I promise."

"I know," I whispered.

A few more thrusts and Alex tensed up, grunting out his orgasm. His feet scrambled at the sheets for traction, pressing himself deep into me. I held him tight, rocking with him as he came.

———

A few hours later, after four more orgasms—one more for Alex, three for me—we ate takeaway on my bed, naked.

"It's not my fancy French place, but it'll do," I said, slurping up a noodle.

Alex looked at me with such fondness. "Who would have thought I'd have Nikki Kozlova slurping my noodles?"

I almost choked, and Alex laughed.

"Actually," he began, setting his food down, "I wanted to show you my new camera."

I paused in digging for my next noodle. "Wait," I said, dropping the carton down in my lap. Surely, I hadn't heard him correctly. "What did you say?"

His face brightened. "I got a new camera. I was hoping you could take a look at it and tell me what you think, maybe give me some pointers."

I gathered the sheets at my waist, my heart pounding and dread settling in my stomach. "Show me."

Alex left the room, retrieving the small bag he'd left by the door. No longer distracted by a handsome date, I could see it for what it was, a camera bag. He unzipped it, pulling out a Sony, the latest model that had sold out instantly and had a months-long waiting list. I hadn't even planned on upgrading yet, as my camera was only a few years old, but I'd thought about it. Was tempted by it. And here was a shiny brand-new model flush with the latest stabilizing technology and an even higher f-stop.

I reached out reverently, and Alex placed the camera in my hands. I zoomed in and out, the motions of the lens smooth and graceful. I flipped it on, pivoted the screen, tested the buttons, even took the lens cap off and took a few shots, aiming randomly around my flat.

It was a gorgeous camera.

And once again, Alex was busting out of the gates bigger, better, faster, all the things I wasn't. Sure, I could upgrade my camera to match his, but what was the point? I knew Alex wouldn't be taking trips with me, but the next time we'd travel together, it'd be a complete competition. Even with my experience, Alex would hire an instructor, take a course, devote himself entirely to the camera and chasing the shot.

I could picture this future, us fighting for position to get the best shot, his brilliance leading him to all kinds of creative ideas. Then we'd compare notes, and he'd gloat—sure, my shots were great, but his were better.

Worst of all, this was my career. It was still a budding one, but I just couldn't stand the thought of being bested at yet another thing, especially something I wanted to make my living at.

"Alex, what are you going to do with a camera?"

He shrugged. "I don't know. I thought we could take some courses together, maybe do some photography challenges. Who knows, you might finally get me interested in my Instagram account."

I closed my eyes. "Why do you do this?"

He responded, and I could hear the bafflement in his voice. "Do what?"

"I'm a photographer, Alex. Look, I know I didn't say anything before, but this is exactly why I didn't, and you went and did it anyway!"

"Well, you didn't say anything, but I kind of figured it out with the big camera and whatnot."

"No, Alex." I opened my eyes and looked at him. I could feel my lip starting to quiver, and bit it, trying to hide my frustration. "I'm a photographer—as in, that trip was comped, and I was getting paid to be there. This is what I do now."

His face shifted to deeper puzzlement. "On Instagram?"

"That's how it started, with Ion. He was tired of the photography and trying to figure out how to self-promote on Instagram, so I took over his account. That was me behind the camera, me posting and figuring out hashtags and Stories and how to position him to grow his fan base. And I'm really good at it. Not just the marketing, but the camera."

Alex watched me. "I didn't mean that you aren't good at it."

"I know that. And I know there's photographers out there who are better than me, but you, you pick up everything I do, and you rub it in my face and make me feel small and inadequate."

"I don't—" Alex started.

"Yeah, you do. Do you remember when I ran the London Marathon to fundraise for that children's charity? I went around our friend group and my mother's social clubs to get people to pitch in. I did months of training and then, suddenly, you're running the race, too, and you tripled what I raised, and then, finally, we ran the race, and you came in so much faster than I did." A tear slipped down my face, and I brushed it away. "And then I had been talking to Coach Johnston to train me for that regatta in Malta, and suddenly he emails me back with, 'I will be unable to make a commitment to you. I've been hired by another team to coach.' And shocker, it was you. It sounds small and dumb when I say it out loud, but you always dig your way into my favorite things, and it's honestly, just not that much fun when someone's always coming along and besting me. Over and over again."

I sat up a little straighter, my anger building. "You're always there, Alex, and I won't let you take this away from me too."

Alex's jaw had set, a flush rising in his cheeks. "Right, okay, you don't want me to take up photography, fine." He turned and, despite his anger, carefully packed the camera away.

"Don't turn this on me to make me the bad guy. You're always swooping in, and you're always better."

"That's not… that's not what this is about, Nikki. I'm not trying to take your career away. I just . . . I thought we could do this together."

"By beating me all the time? You're competitive and so bloody awful about it. That is not a good plan."

His jaw tightened further, and I could see that I'd hurt

him. "Fine, forget it, Nikki. I'll return the camera. I'll leave you alone to do your own thing, okay?"

"Fine." I crossed my arms in front of my chest. We stared at each other for a beat, and then Alex started to pull his clothes on.

"You make it sound like I'm awful to spend time with. Why would you want to be around me when I ruin things for you?" His voice was clipped, and he dressed faster, barely buttoning his shirt before pulling on his socks.

"Stop ruining things for me, then."

"So, what, I'll just work constantly?"

He said it as if there was no alternative, as if his options were work or compete. As if, without the pleasure of competition, he didn't want me playing in his sandbox.

"Right, go be workaholic Alex. Let's just pretend this whole trip never happened. Forget the date." Tears were filling up my eyes, threatening to spill down, and I clenched my jaw. If I could just get him out the door. I didn't want him to see me cry.

Alex stood up, his jaw clenched, and his fingers shook in anger. "If that's what you want, fine. Goodnight, Nikki."

And he was gone. The door slammed shut, and I burst into tears.

SEVENTEEN

THE YOGA RETREAT WAS GOING WONDERFULLY FROM A photography perspective. I was in Sri Lanka for four days, but the work had really only taken up two. I had wandered around the retreat, taking photos of everything I could find: sun salutations on a hill overlooking rows of winding tea bushes, serene pools of water with lush jungle providing shade while people bent into downward dog, and small basins of water with flower petals floating on the surface laid out in delicate patterns. My SD card filled with photos of serenity and calm every day, and I dumped it out every night.

During the day, I could focus on work, but at night I lay in bed and thought of Alex. It was so different here. Instead of a king-sized bed, I slept on a double and wondered how it would be to share this smaller space with Alex. I'd imagine how it would feel to wake up tangled in him.

Instead of rowdy, family-style dinners, it was quiet meals often eaten on my own, fresh fruits, smoothies, and vegan dishes. No wild game steaks like at the lodge.

Alex was so competitive. It would never work between us. He needed someone to compete with him tooth and nail. Someone with more drive and ambition than me.

It was a vacation fling. A temporary insanity. Why would I be falling in love with the guy who antagonized me at every turn?

But I couldn't let it go. What if I'd just told him outright to stop competing with me? What if I'd told him how much it meant to me to do my own thing?

When we'd just been rivals, it was fine. It hadn't mattered.

But a nagging part of my brain was telling me that Alex, my boyfriend, my lover, this new Alex, would have been different.

———

My Uber driver pulled up outside of my flat near midnight. My flight home had been delayed, twice, and I was exhausted with jet lag. I grabbed my backpack before thanking him and pushing the door open. I stopped, halfway out of the car, when I spotted a shadow hunched over on my front stairs. Boxes were piled around him, an arm thrown over one of them. His head was tilted back against the wall, mouth slightly open while he slept.

"Miss?" My driver leaned over the front seat, peering out the window at Alex on my steps. "Do you need me to call the cops?"

"No, it's fine, thanks," I said, shaking myself back into motion. I hefted my bag over my shoulder and shut the car door.

Alex startled at the noise and blinked, my front light casting harsh shadows across his face as he woke up, scrubbing his cheeks and looking around.

"Nikki," he rasped out. "Hi."

I carefully climbed my steps around the mound of boxes. *Sony*, one box read. *Lowepro*, another. All original boxes for camera gear.

"What are you doing here, Alex?"

"I wanted to give you this stuff." He gestured around.

I nudged one of the boxes nearby with a lens on the side and felt the heavy weight inside. "You didn't want to just return it?"

He shook his head.

"Alright," I said, unlocking my door. "Help me get the boxes in."

We propped my door open and carried the boxes through to my kitchen table, passing each other in the hallway. Alex looked rough, but I supposed sleeping on a door stoop would do that. He was wearing trousers and a dress shirt, which had rumpled from a day in the office and waiting for me. His hair stuck up everywhere, his eyes were tired, his stubble outrageous, and he looked like shit. Part of me rejoiced; he deserved it.

Part of me wondered if I looked any better.

Eventually, we had a pile of camera gear, three or four boxes deep, on my table. It was way more gear than I needed. I'd have to figure out what to do with it all.

"This is the last one," I said as I came in from the door. Alex changed course, and instead of leaving my place, he stood to the side as I stacked the box.

When I turned around, Alex was gripping the back of one of my chairs, watching me. I expected him to make an excuse and leave, getting back to his workaholic lifestyle so I could go back to avoiding him. Maybe he'd even start avoiding me.

That thought didn't feel as good as I'd hoped.

"Nikki, I am so sorry."

My heart leapt a little, nerves kicking up as the words settled over me. It felt good, a little vindication, but I was still wary. "What are you apologizing for?"

Alex ran a hand through his hair. "Can we talk? I had hoped... I was waiting for you to get home so we could talk. I didn't want to just post these things to you."

Despite it being late and jet lag weighing me down, I wanted him to stay.

I stepped over to the couch and settled in one corner, gesturing to the other. "How did you know when I was getting home?"

"My mum asked your mum."

My lips twitched. "Of course."

"They are eternally optimistic about us, even after I told my mum everything."

I folded my legs underneath me and waited. Alex rubbed his hands together and drew out a breath. "Did you know my parents nearly divorced?"

I blinked at him. That wasn't what I was expecting him to say. "Ummm....when?"

"Our last year of school." He shifted his weight on the couch and scratched at his nail. "Pretty close to that party when we kissed, actually."

I thought back to the days where I'd gone over to the Boyds' residence and seen his parents. They both doted on him; Alex and his mum had so much in common, and his stay-at-home dad had raised him. I'd always been jealous of his tight-knit family. "They didn't, though. What happened?"

"My mum's a workaholic, just like me." He gave a self-deprecating laugh. "Sometimes I think I'm too much like her. I have her looks, her work habits, and someday I'll have her job." Alex leaned forward, placing his elbows on his knees and rubbing his face before continuing. "When we moved to the city, Mum was working a lot more. She had more pressure, more employees, more responsibilities. More stress. On the other side, I was growing up and getting independent. I didn't need my dad in the same way. I remember coming home some nights from tutoring or your house and finding him alone in the study, the house dark and quiet around him."

"Because your mum was always working."

He nodded. "Mum always had strong priorities. And my father had slipped down on the list. Something snapped, and Dad had had enough. They separated for three weeks or so, trying to figure out how to move forward."

"What did they decide to do?"

"They compromised, changed their schedules. Mum committed to taking lunches off once a week to have a long lunch with Dad. He vowed to be more present around her office. Now that I could be on my own, Dad was free to come to more evening work functions. And with my dad having more free time, Mum asked him what he wanted to do with himself. And he said he wanted to try cycling. So they did it together."

I couldn't help myself, and I snorted. "Your mum is just as competitive as you are. I can't imagine how your dad handled that."

Alex ignored my laugh. "He loved it. He's competitive, too, you know, and it really got them to spend a lot of time together. They'd spend weekends on the road, and for a while, conversations about bikes and races and group rides were what I came home to. Now it's more along the lines of yoga and swimming, vacationing on *Themis*, that kind of thing."

"I'm glad that they sorted it out. That must have been tough for you. But I don't understand what this has to do with us."

Alex clasped his hands together and met my eyes. "I *am* a workaholic. I always will be. I love my job. But I want to love someone. I want to love *you*, Nikki. And I want you to know that I will always make time for you in my life, I will always be interested in what you are interested in, I will always listen when you talk about your dreams, your hobbies"—he gestured to the pile of camera gear—"your career. I realize that I've gone about it all wrong now. It's not something I can force my way into. I just wanted to spend time with you.

That's what I tried to do, with the running, the sailing, the camera, and for that, I am truly sorry."

Carefully, Alex reached over and took my hand, cupping it in both of his and giving me a little squeeze. "I love my mum, but I never want to lose sight of what's really important. I promise that I'll let you have your own career. I didn't realize what you were doing, and I want you to know how much I admire the work you've done."

I looked at our joined hands. "You didn't know because I didn't tell you. I even lied to you, which I regret, and I'm sorry for that too. I worried that you would make me want to give up photography too. I'm just not competitive, and I don't want to compete with you. I want to love doing something and stick with it because it makes me happy."

"And that's photography?" he asked, eyes flickering to the boxes on my table.

"Yes, it is. I love it. And I'm good at it."

Alex's grin turned sheepish. "I did find your Instagram account."

"Oh?"

"Yeah, the lodge shared one of your photos and gave you credit for it. I looked through your profile and then your portfolio. You are really good, Nikki." He squeezed my hand again.

I let my fingers slip out from his and turned to look over the couch at the boxes. "So you bought a bunch of expensive gear just so you could learn how to be a photographer with me?"

He grimaced. "Yeah. When you say it out loud like that, it sounds ridiculous. So privileged."

"You know," I said, turning back to him, "there's a lot of different types of photography. You could do portraits or fashion or something else."

"To be honest, I never had much interest in photography. It was really all about you."

"Is that true with everything else? Sailing? Running?"

"Sailing was fun," he admitted. "It's encouraged me to learn from the crew on *Themis*, and now, when I visit, I take out one of the sailing dinghies and zip around. But running." He shuddered. "I am never running again if I can help it. I didn't find out you were participating in the marathon until two months beforehand, and I did a stupid training schedule that wasn't nearly enough."

We smiled at each other, and I leaned my head on the back of the couch.

"I walked bowlegged for days afterward."

I snorted. "Serves you right. I trained for six months!"

Alex let his smile fade and sat up. "Right, well. I should get going." He stood up, and I followed him toward the door. "I've said my piece, and…" His shoulders climbed toward his ears as he turned to face me while I opened the door. "I hope you forgive me."

It wasn't a question, but I answered it anyway. "I do. We're very different, Alex, but I can understand why you did what you did. I appreciate the apology."

His shoulders settled as he stepped out into the night, and his head tilted back, looking up at the night sky glowing from the city lights. "Not at all like the stars we saw in South Africa, are they?"

"No," I agreed. "Everything looks a little different now."

He sighed, dropping his eyes down to his feet as he took the stairs down. "Goodnight, Nikki."

When he hit the bottom step, I called out, "Hey, Alex?"

He turned, the light catching his face and highlighting the hopefulness.

"I have a few weeks until my next trip. Take me out to dinner next week."

His smile lit up the shadows. "Yes, ma'am."

EPILOGUE

A FEW MONTHS LATER, I HEFTED MY BACKPACK UP HIGHER AND adjusted the straps as I walked through the arrivals terminal of Heathrow. I was returning from a weekend festival in Bearsden, where I'd had a press pass and a partnership with the local tourist board. It had been a whirlwind—I really should have suggested an additional day or two, but I knew they were on a tight budget.

As most travelers peeled off to the baggage claim, I slipped through the exit and pulled out my phone. Alex was picking me up from the airport, and I needed to text him which door I was coming out of.

"Nikki!"

I looked up at my name. Alex stood off to the right side, holding a bouquet of flowers and wearing a big smile.

"Hey, honey! What a surprise!" I threw my arms around him, and he carefully wove one hand between me and the backpack to hold me close.

We pulled back just enough for a quick peck before moving out of the way and out toward the parking lot. Alex held my hand tightly, asking how my flight had been and if I was hungry while he navigated the car away from the airport.

Dating Alex had been a balancing act for both of us. He emailed me a list of suggested dates, from a wine tasting to a polo club, which I emailed back with, "I don't need you to entertain me...in that way."

We did go out on dates. Lovely nights out where we just talked and enjoyed each other's company. When I was gone on trips, Alex worked hard, staying late at the office and adjusting his schedule. When I was in town, he got more flexible until we were spending weekends at my house, both of us working on our laptops occasionally but mostly spending our time naked and in bed. Once he'd learned to relax and not try to force things too much, Alex was a bad influence. He was always pulling me back into bed, showing me his affection with physical touch, as well as our quality time together.

Instead of pulling up to the pavement outside my house, Alex parked and followed me up to my door. I checked my watch; it was two o'clock.

"Don't you need to get back to the office?" I said as I unlocked my door.

"I took the rest of the day off today."

"Oh?" I slumped my backpack against the entryway and kicked off my shoes. It felt good to be home.

"Yes," he said, coming up behind me and wrapping his arms around my waist. "I want to make sure you know how much you mean to me."

A slow smile twisted my lips. "How much do I mean to you?"

He laughed and curled around me. I looked down and saw his feet between mine, my socks between his dress shoes.

"Every time I kiss you, I can't help but think of all the times I wanted to kiss you. And it goes so far back. I wanted to kiss you when you were cleaning graffiti off my locker, and I wanted to kiss you every time the bellends in our school called you Tits McGhee and you let it roll off your back. I wanted to kiss you when you crossed the finish line of the marathon and when we were at the starting line of the regatta. When we yelled at each other with fondant between our toes.

"And now," he said, taking a deep breath, "when I think of all those things, I don't just want to kiss you. I want to tell you that I love you, and I always have. And I wish I could erase everything I did to make you upset rather than in love with me."

"I don't," I said immediately. "You said to me before that we wouldn't have known what to do with each other back then." I turned around in his arms, grabbing the sides of his shirt, gripping him close, and pressing our bodies together. I looked up at him, his face solemn but his eyes shining. "And you were right. But now, Alex, I know what to do with you. I know how to love you."

And I kissed him.

It took a week in the wild to push us together. Over the years, we'd matured, we'd grown.

And now I was truly, wildly happy.

THE END

Also by Liz Alden:

<u>The Love and Wanderlust Series</u>
The Night in Lover's Bay (free prequel short story)
The Fling in Panama
The Slow Burn in Polynesia
The Second Chance in the Mediterranean
The Rival in South Africa (standalone novella)
The Player in New Zealand
The Best Friend in Indonesia (free standalone short story)

<u>Aged Like Fine Wine Series</u>
Rosé with My Fake Fiancé
Riesling with My Roommate
Prosecco with My Professor
Cava with My Colleague

<u>Holiday Retellings Series</u>
Nutcracker with Benefits
Frosty Proximity

<u>Wanderlust Resort Series</u>
Beach Boss (free standalone short story)
Beach Resolution
Put it in Beach Mode

<u>Standalones</u>
The Boudoir Arrangement

ACKNOWLEDGMENTS

This past year has been a boon for both my writing and reading friendships. I get the pleasure of calling some of my favorite authors friends, and that's rather baffling. I've gotten to meet readers and writers who were once digital friends IRL, and for that, I am very thankful.

Thank you to my editing team, Sarah Pesce of Lopt & Cropt and Lisa Matsumura, and to Elizabeth Stokes for the amazing cover.

And as always, a big thank-you to my husband, who encouraged me so much from day one, and my parents, all five of them, who supported this book in one way or another.

ABOUT LIZ ALDEN

Liz Alden is a digital nomad. Most of the time, she's on her sailboat, but sometimes she's in Texas. She knows exactly how big the world is—having sailed around it—and exactly how small it is, having bumped into friends worldwide. She's been a dishwasher, an engineer, a CEO, and occasionally gets paid to write or sail.

Follow Liz:
LizAlden.com

9 781954 705227